A
Crossworder's
Delight

Crossword Mysteries by Nero Blanc

THE CROSSWORD MURDER
TWO DOWN
THE CROSSWORD CONNECTION
A CROSSWORD TO DIE FOR
A CROSSWORDER'S HOLIDAY
CORPUS DE CROSSWORD
A CROSSWORDER'S GIFT
ANATOMY OF A CROSSWORD
WRAPPED UP IN CROSSWORDS
ANOTHER WORD FOR MURDER
A CROSSWORDER'S DELIGHT

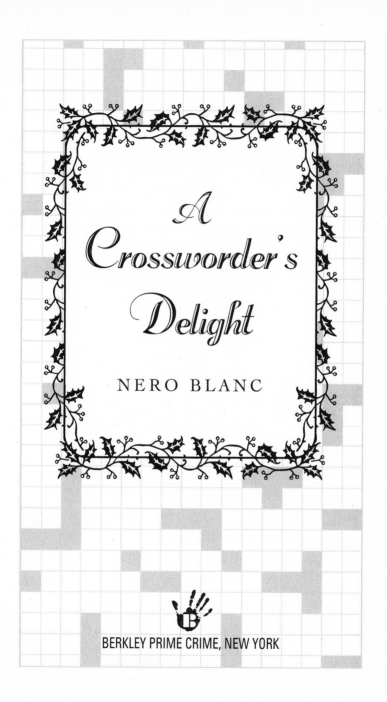

A Crossworder's Delight

NERO BLANC

BERKLEY PRIME CRIME, NEW YORK

THE BERKLEY PUBLISHING GROUP
Published by the Penguin Group
Penguin Group (USA) Inc.
375 Hudson Street, New York, New York 10014, USA
Penguin Group (Canada), 90 Eglinton Avenue East, Suite 700, Toronto, Ontario M4P 2Y3, Canada
(a division of Pearson Penguin Canada Inc.)
Penguin Books Ltd., 80 Strand, London WC2R 0RL, England
Penguin Group Ireland, 25 St. Stephen's Green, Dublin 2, Ireland (a division of Penguin Books Ltd.)
Penguin Group (Australia), 250 Camberwell Road, Camberwell, Victoria 3124, Australia
(a division of Pearson Australia Group Pty. Ltd.)
Penguin Books India Pvt. Ltd., 11 Community Centre, Panchsheel Park, New Delhi—110 017, India
Penguin Group (NZ), Cnr. Airborne and Rosedale Roads, Albany, Auckland 1310, New Zealand
(a division of Pearson New Zealand Ltd.)
Penguin Books (South Africa) (Pty.) Ltd., 24 Sturdee Avenue, Rosebank, Johannesburg 2196,
South Africa

Penguin Books Ltd., Registered Offices: 80 Strand, London WC2R 0RL, England

This is an original publication of The Berkley Publishing Group.

First edition: October 2005

Library of Congress Cataloging-in-Publication Data

Blanc, Nero.
    A crossworder's delight / Nero Blanc.
        p. cm.
    ISBN 0-425-20656-4
    1. Polycrates, Rosco (Fictitious character)—Fiction. 2. Graham, Belle (Ficititious character)—
Fiction. 3. Crossword puzzle makers—Fiction. 4. Crossword puzzles—Fiction. 5. Massachusetts—
Fiction. I. Title.

PS3552.L365C78 2005
813'.54—dc22

                                                                            2005047835

PRINTED IN THE UNITED STATES OF AMERICA

10   9   8   7   6   5   4   3   2   1

GREETINGS FROM NERO BLANC

Dear Friends,

What would holidays and family gatherings be without special recipes passed along and shared? Our own memories of childhood are irrevocably connected to the wonderful smells of baking that filled relatives' homes when we arrived for a visit: pies and angel-food cakes made proudly from scratch, the dough carefully kneaded and rolled, the egg whites beaten by hand.

In the spirit of those happy and bygone days, we dedicate this book to the memory of Cordelia's mother, Cordelia Frances Fenton Biddle, and to her mother, Mary Frances Higgins Fenton, who made the very best fudge in the world.

And we also give many thanks to Midge Walter and her son, Tony, of Lore's Chocolates in Philadelphia. As current residents of the city, we can promise you that holidays aren't the same without numerous samplings of Lore's wares. Tony provided technical information as well as a glimpse into the workings of a true confectionery shop. If you're in Philadelphia, be sure to visit their store on Seventh Street. It's a pure delight!

Please remember that our website www.CrosswordMysteries .com has puzzles to download, and that we do love getting your letters.

Cordelia and Steve

One

TRADITION and *traditional* were key words at the Paul Revere Inn. *Historic, venerable, quaint,* even *revered* might vie for the prize, but the notion of the hostelry and eatery as being paramount to the timeless *traditions* of New-castle always won out. Especially on the day after Thanksgiving, when the annual Holiday Decoration Competition was in full swing, and this coastal Massa-chusetts city's volunteer organizations descended en masse upon the rambling old building, dead-set on transforming it into exuberant holiday mode—a la the late eighteenth century.

The rivalry between the competing groups was fierce, culminating at the inn's Solstice Dinner, when the civic association whose members displayed the most wizardry with garlands of greenery, cranberries strung on thread, pomanders of orange and clove, hand-dipped candles, barley-sugar figures, and gingerbread creatures was awarded the coveted silver Revere bowl. It was a contest with a capital *C,* and a noted lack of reverence permeated the air.

"Coming through, ladies and gentlemen. Coming though." This regal voice belonged to Sara Crane Briephs, presiding "Queen mum" of Sisters-in-Stitches, a church sewing group that had lost the prize for four hard-luck years in a row. In Sara's hands was a large hat box containing copper and tin ornaments in the shapes of stars and snowflakes. They were old and valuable and had resided in the attic of her ancestral home, White-caps, for as long as anyone could remember. "We'll tie them with bows and hang them from the pewter chandelier. None of the other groups have anything to remotely equal them. If I'd only remembered these things last year. . . ."

As she spoke, Sara jostled her way through the throng crowded outside the inn's front parlor, the room being the one assigned to the Sisters. The parlor was notoriously difficult to decorate, its focal point being a much-beloved icon: a signed original printing of Henry Wadsworth Longfellow's poem "Paul Revere's Ride." It was Longfellow's ode to Massachusetts's hero of the Revolutionary War that had inspired the grandparents of the inn's current owners to change the hostelry's name when they'd purchased the place in the early 1920s. The treasured artifact had hung in the same spot for close to eighty years. Needless to say, its large gilt frame didn't make for easy decorative magic.

Martha Leonetti shook her head as she watched Sara enter; Martha was the only other Sister present in the parlor, and she observed the hat box and its owner with an habitually jaundiced eye. Head waitress at Lawson's Coffee Shop in the city's downtown commercial center, Martha prided herself on her worldly wisdom and sassy candor. She knew the life stories of all her regular customers, what they habitually ordered, and/or wanted to order but didn't. And she wasn't adverse to providing "much-needed advice" about diets and love lives and career choices and family squabbles, or dishing out the latest dirt right along with the home fries. She would have seemed the antithesis of the patrician Sara, but the two had formed such a bond of friendship that they often appeared to be each other's alter ego. The noted exception was that Martha had sported the same aggressively blonde beehive hairdo for the past three decades while Sara, at eighty-plus, had a coiffure that was a natural snowy white.

"I don't know, Sara. Seems to me like guests will keep bashing their heads on your do-dads. And that could lose us points, big time. The ceilings are way too low in here; and with everyone gawking at the poem and all, crowding around to read it and what have you, well, someone could get hurt. . . . Better put your gee-gaws out of the way—maybe up on the mantle or hang them on velvet ribbons over the windows."

"But if we put them on the mantle, they'll simply disappear within all those clusters of greens, Martha."

"Didn't you tell us gals that we should keep things 'subtle' this year? Wasn't that the new stratagem?"

"Subtle doesn't mean hidden," Sara countered loftily.

"Hmmmph," Martha sniffed. She was standing in her stocking feet atop a step stool as she tried to drape a window with a loop of cedar garland. Reaching up to push the prickly pieces in place, her body looked dangerously unbalanced and unsteady. "If I want to know the meaning of a word, I'll ask our resident linguistic expert. . . . Heya, Belle, get your tush in here, pronto," Martha bellowed toward the door. "Will you please explain to Her Highness here that I'm not suggesting subterfuge when it comes to displaying her prize ornaments?"

Belle Graham was carrying a coiled garland of white pine as she walked into the parlor; its sap had left dark, sticky marks on her hands that had then been transferred to her face as she'd pushed her corn-silk–colored hair aside. Despite the romantic given name of Annabella, she wasn't adept at maintaining a ladylike pose. And she never, ever called herself Annabella or Anna. Being the crossword puzzle editor for one of Newcastle's daily newspapers, *The Evening Crier,* had produced one too many gibes about being "Ms. Anna-Graham." "What are you two quibbling about now?" Belle shook her head and smiled as she spoke.

"Martha's insisting my handsome family ornaments should be all but hidden like snakes in the grass."

"I am not, your ladyship! I'm only saying those pointy ends might prove dangerous when dangling down in the middle of the room. Poke some tall dude or dudess in the noggin, or scratch some follicly challenged baldy's pate."

"And where does 'subterfuge' enter into this argument?" Belle asked.

"It's Martha's term, not mine," was Sara quick retort. "As you know, I've been advocating subtilty, because last year we made the terrible mistake of—"

"Ah yes, the *subliminal* approach to decorating." Belle laughed. "A bit *subversive,* don't you think, Sara? *Sub rosa, surreptitious, sly*—"

"I prefer the word *stealthy,* dear." Sara also laughed. As Belle's self-styled surrogate grandmother, she enjoyed tinkering with language as much as Newcastle's celebrated word game editor. "Creating artful interiors requires a certain craftiness. What else is *trompe l'oeil* but a means to trick the eye? A wave of the wand—or in this case, the glue gun—and then poof! Now you see it, now you don't."

"You ladies aren't planning on making things disappear, are you?" Stanley Hatch asked as he strode into the

room. Stan was the owner of Hatch's Hardware, and an
"honorary" member of Sisters-in-Stitches. He supplied
brawn (in his mid fifties, he was still slim, tall, and
muscular), as well as the all-important tools of the
craftsman's trade. "Because, if any of the inn's pricey antiques were to take a powder . . . well, let's just say it
wouldn't be likely that we'd be invited back next year to
compete."

"What a ridiculous notion, Stanley," was Sara's
amused response. "We're here to *add* to the Marz twins'
furnishings, not subtract from them." Then Sara
abruptly shifted her focus. "Give Martha a hand with
those swags above the windows, will you, dear boy? I'm
afraid if she tries to reach any higher, she'll take a tum-
ble. And crutches certainly won't aid in her labors at
Lawson's."

But this request met with unexpected hesitation
from both the principals. Wisecracking Martha grew
suddenly shy and quiet. Stan made a move to help her
from the stepladder, then awkwardly withdrew his hand
as Martha clamored heavily down on her own, finally
making a show of searching for her shoes. She never
once glanced in Stanley's direction. Their behavior was
no different than that of a couple of smitten fourteen-
year-olds. It did not go unnoticed.

Sara and Belle shared a meaningful look. Stanley was
a widower; Martha was also single. The two were des-
tined for each other—at least, that was their friends'

opinion. Why it was taking the pair so long to act upon this obvious fact was beyond anyone's comprehension, although it was Sara who felt the most frustrated at the duo's lack of gumption. She was the one who'd originally conceived of the notion of forming a couple from two lonely people. "Your shoes are under the wing chair," she told Martha with unaccustomed chilliness, "where you left them, dear."

Martha dutifully retrieved her pumps while Sara released a hearty sigh; and Stan, in order to cover his own embarrassment, walked over to the wall where the Longfellow hung.

"*A cry of defiance and not of fear,*" Stanley read aloud from the final stanza,

> "*A voice in the darkness, a knock at the door,*
> "*And a word that shall echo forevermore!*
> "*For, borne on the night-wind of the Past,*
> "*Through all our history, to the last,*
> "*In the hour of darkness, and peril, and need,*
> "*The people will waken to listen and hear*
> "*The hurrying hoof beats of that steed,*
> "*And the midnight message of Paul Revere.*"

He stood, studying the words. "We still need stirring messages like that, don't we?"

"More than ever before," Sara replied with feeling, then added a brisk, "You read it beautifully, Stanley," as if she were afraid of revealing too much of her weaker nature.

"Yes, you did, Stan," Martha echoed in a hushed and unfamiliar murmur.

"Well, you're the one who gave me that Kipling at the Secret Santa exchange last year," was his pleased response. "And without knowing how much I liked his poems. 'If' always reminds me of my granddad. . . . Funny how that is."

But Martha's reply to this obvious invitation to further conversation was to avoid Stanley's glance, duck her head, and mumble a businesslike "We'd better get back to work. The other Sisters will be arriving any sec, and this room's going to get as crazy busy as Lawson's on a Saturday morning snowfall."

"If you don't need any further verbal explications, I'll leave you at it, then," Belle said, propping the coiled garland against the hearth. "You know me around glue guns and such. . . ."

"Don't want to fuse your house keys and car keys together like you did last year, huh?" Martha jibed.

Belle chuckled. "If everyone hadn't been forced to stop what they were doing and help me out of my mess, the Sisters would have made a better showing."

"That's sweet of you, dear," was Sara's soothing reply. "However, I don't believe your accident caused us to lose. I feel our design approach was lacking in sufficient vision."

"Which is exactly what's gonna happen if we hang those pointed pretties of yours at eye-level, Sara. *Lack of vision* for some guest would definitely put us once again in last place."

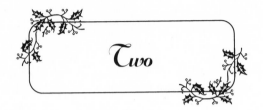

Two

EAVING Martha, Stanley, and Sara, Belle continued her tour of the building, greeting other competition participants as they bustled around the low-beamed reception areas, the three intimate dining rooms, the formal staircase, and the rear parlor. Fires were lit in every hearth; the waitstaff, dressed in period costumes, lent an air of authenticity to the scene while the paying guests seemed caught up in the festive spirit. Many were aiding the Newcastle regulars. The instant camaraderie seemed to Belle the very quintessence of the holidays, and she was smiling happily as she climbed the stairs to the second-floor bedrooms, then to the third floor with its dormer windows and views of the now-frozen lawn and garden. There she walked down the hall, revelling in the sense of past and present joined together, before she came to the half-open door of a room converted to office use where she overheard a *sotto voce* spat between Morgan and Mitchell Marz, the twins who now owned the inn.

In their sixties, the brothers were physically identical: two sturdy men with expanding waistlines, two full heads of salt-and-pepper hair, and a shared penchant for brightly hued turtleneck sweaters. Where business was concerned, however, they had a fundamental difference of opinion.

"Mitch's kitsch!" Morgan was grumbling. This was a common expression of his, just as it was standard practice for him to gripe about the valuable antique furnishings his brother insisted on keeping *in situ,* and that Morgan believed should be sold. "Have you looked at our insurance premiums recently, Mitch? Have you? We simply can't afford to keep all this—"

"It's not *kitsch,* Morgan. If it were, insuring it wouldn't be so expensive!"

"Oh, for Pete's sake!"

But Mitchell's gentle tone overrode his brother's exacerbated interruption. "And for another thing, it's our legacy. Our grandparents wanted the inn to have—"

"You can't keep wallowing with ghosts forever!"

"I'm not wallowing, Morgan. It's what they wished."

"And what about our mother, is it what she wanted, too?"

"Morgan, we both know she worked very, very hard during the time when Dad was—"

"My point exactly! Now, please don't start with—"

"When Dad was off during the war," Mitchell continued as if his brother hadn't spoken; although his desire to make his point, combined with a modesty that could verge on shyness, caused his words to stumble—a trait his more forceful twin didn't share. "B-b-because she wanted the inn to continue to look the same as it had when—"

"Oh, stop. You don't know that, Mitch. In fact, I'll bet the opposite was true, and she wanted to chuck all these historic references, and streamline the—"

"That's simply not true, Morgan! It's . . . it's—"

"Okay. My mistake. Maybe she didn't. Maybe she was perfectly happy with the status quo. That's not the point. It's the cost of protecting these pieces I'm objecting to. Besides, what if we had a fire, or a theft? What if one of these antiques you love so much should—?"

"B-b-but our guests come here *because* of these articles." Mitchell's tone was disbelieving. "History is the Revere Inn's strong suit. Stepping inside our doors is like . . . it's like walking into the past."

Morgan groaned in frustration. "I'm not disagreeing with the traditional approach, Mitch. You know I'm not. I realize that's what attracts our clientele: Queen Anne and Shaker furniture, and so forth . . . but we could have the same design appeal without the price tag of maintaining genuine—"

"Well, you can't get more *traditional* than real antiques, Morgan. Besides . . ."

Belle moved on and the Marz brothers' argument eventually vanished into the half-light of the narrow corridor whose path wrapped around unexpected corners and climbed surprise single-step rises.

At last, she came to a room that was far from the hubbub, a cubbyhole of a spot lined with shelves on which sat forgotten books and board games and wooden jigsaw puzzles that were undoubtedly missing crucial pieces. The room smelled pleasantly of age. She scanned the library, wondering if Mitchell—in one of his many antiquing forays—had added any unusual finds, but nothing exciting caught her eye. Not for a moment, anyway. Then she spotted a volume that was slimmer than the rest, an unprepossessing black book no thicker than a pamphlet. Belle carefully withdrew it from the shelf and opened it.

To my dear daughter who so loves chocolate.
These are for you from your loving Mama.

The pages were crossword puzzles. The clues and solutions belonged to recipes, but none of the word games were completed. In fact, it looked as though the book hadn't been opened since "Mama" had penned those old-fashioned and curlicued lines.

Belle hurried back to the brothers and presented them with the little volume. But Mitchell looked blank when asked from whence the book had come.

"I don't have a clue, I'm afraid, Belle. . . . Maybe it was . . . maybe it was in a box of books I bought at a yard sale or a second-hand store."

"Which he does on a regular basis," Morgan offered with a beleaguered sigh. "Snaps them up as if there were no tomorrow—all by color and size. Books by the yard, *from* the yard. Next stop would be the dumpster if it weren't for my dear brother here."

"No one throws away books, Morgan. They're . . . they're—"

Belle interrupted before this new altercation could escalate. "And this one doesn't look remotely familiar?"

"Was it with the other black ones?" Mitchell asked, and she nodded.

"See what I mean?" Morgan shook his head. "It's a decor thing. There are the black ones, the red ones, the blue—"

"I'm afraid I can't help you," Mitch continued. "I must have pulled them out of a box and slid them onto the shelf. Obviously, if I'd opened this particular book, I w-would have thought of you immediately."

But weren't you even curious what those volumes contained? Belle wanted to ask, but didn't. Collectors were quirky folk. Some were inspired by the purely visual; some needed the reassuring touch of their possessions; some liked to discuss the minutest details of history and other data; for some it was an investment only.

"May I borrow this?" Belle asked.

It was Morgan who answered. "Just take the thing, Belle. There's no need to return it."

But his brother regarded the book with covetous eyes. "Why don't you *borrow* it for the time being. Then we'll see. But may I ask what you intend to do with it?"

Find the owner, Belle almost answered, but she knew how foolish that would sound. A box of discarded books found in a yard sale: what was the chance of tracing its history? "I'd just like to try my hand at the puzzles," she said instead.

Holiday Slay Ride

Melt over hot water: 2 tbsp. butter; 2 oz. unsweetened chocolate

Sift together: ¾ cup *29-Down;* 1 cup flour; 2 tsp. *9-Down;* ⅛ *21-Down*

Combine the chocolate and flour mixtures

Stir in: ½ cup milk; ½ tsp. vanilla extract

Pour batter into buttered baking dish (about 9×9 inches)

Mix, then scatter over batter: ½ cup *52-Across;* ½ cup *29-Down;* 4 tbs cocoa

Gently pour 1 ½ cups *3-Down* over the whole mixture

Bake at 350 degrees for forty minutes until a delicious crust forms on top and the inside is runny.

Serves six, warm or cool . . .

ACROSS

1. Confronts
6. Tulip tuber
10. Poke
14. Maine town
15. On the 26-Across
16. Capital of Italia
17. A Titan
18. Bill
19. News ____
20. Mason jar tops
21. Cagney comedy
23. "Wait a ____!"
24. Gorcey of "Mr. Wise Guy," and others
25. Never in Berlin
26. Indian or Arctic
28. Cpl.'s boss
29. What person
32. M-1s, e.g.
34. Child's noisemaker
35. Slim
36. First Greek letter
37. Discovery of 1930
39. General helper
40. Appealed
41. Door sign
42. Slezak of "Lifeboat"
44. Heading on 26-Across
45. Asta, e.g.
46. Confuse
47. Father's lad
48. Namesakes of Mr. Lincoln
49. Bribe
52. MAMA'S DESSERT
56. Mystical poem
57. Indian princess

58. With, in Paris
59. Hedonist
60. Greek war god
61. Horne of "Stormy Weather"
62. One more time
63. Hardy heroine
64. Makes lace
65. Miss Crawford's husband

DOWN

1. Newborn horses
2. Bandleader Shaw
3. MAMA's DESSERT
4. Namesakes of a Spanish queen
5. "Mayday!"
6. Clown
7. Drug addicts
8. Cordelia's father
9. MAMA's DESSERT
10. Nobel award
11. Newspaper section
12. Bad sign
13. Royal lady
21. MAMA's DESSERT
22. Code sound
24. Gray general?
27. Draped
28. Got off one's feet
29. MAMA's DESSERT
30. Skin
31. Unique
32. Knocks
33. Troubles
34. Snip
35. Statuesque
38. Dope
43. Newspaper revenues

🌴 *Holiday Slay Ride* 🌴

45. Ameche of "Wing and a Prayer"
46. Rope plants
47. Like some chocolates
48. Hollywood negotiator
50. Radio sign
51. Singleton of "Blondie"
52. Scamp

53. Unusual
54. Pocket money
55. Iris locale
56. Anger
59. O'Brien of 21-Across

Three

"I gather you're not planning on getting any shuteye tonight." Rosco Polycrates, Belle's adoring husband, was wearing the plaid flannel bathrobe she'd given him two years ago. He still looked like a fish out of water in it, however, as if an ex-cop turned private investigator who had a Greek heritage and a dark, Mediterranean appeal wasn't supposed to be wandering about in garments typically displayed in catalogs depicting cozy New England hearths, gold-colored canines, and their equally fair-haired human pals cuddling nearby.

"It's getting close to midnight, after all . . ." Rosco raised an exaggerated woolly arm, gesturing toward the blackness of the night sky that lay beyond the windows of Belle's home office; a converted rear porch decorated as a crossworder's fantasy: a wood floor painted in a bold black and white grid, lamp shades pasted with puzzles, the drapes hand-blocked to resemble both clues and solutions.

"You'll note that our neighbors aren't burning the midnight oil," Rosco added. "One can only guess what they might be up to? In fact, I was thinking that we might try to entertain ourselves elsewhere as well. 'Bed' is a word that pops into my mind for some reason. Three letters, down or across: your choice."

Seated at her desk and intent on the anonymous cross-word cookbook, Belle failed to answer her husband—behavior he didn't find surprising because he doubted she'd actually heard him. When she was in "full lexical mode," she was often totally unaware of physical sensations: hunger, cold, human or animal sounds, or the fact that her spine had been twisted into a contortionist's position for longer than she could remember.

He repeated his suggestion while the canine part of the picture went to work: Gabby, an excitable curly gray "wheatoodle" or "poodlier" or "combination-wheaten-terrorist-and-wired-poodle-type," skittered forward to nudge Belle's arm with an insistent, wet-nosed snout; and Kit, a wise and normally self-composed brown and white shepherd mix flopped on the painted floor with a dramatic groan.

Belle finally looked up, although Rosco could see from her distracted gaze that she was trying to find a word or phrase that would best describe her present circumstances. When she was concentrating on one of her puzzles, the rest of the world was often reduced to synonym, antonym, or homonym status. At this moment, he decided that she was probably trying to recall how many Tartans she could name, and what the differences were between a Royal Stewart and a clan MacGregor. "What? What's going on?" she asked him.

"I said, are you thinking of coming to bed anytime this year?"

"Bed?" Belle echoed.

"You know, the warm, cozy piece of furniture upstairs where almost anything is possible?"

"Do you realize, Rosco, that the Scottish Highlanders were forbidden to wear their native dress after the rebellion of 1745? Absolutely forbidden by acts of Parliament, whose members believed that the clans would again rise up to fight the English if they were permitted to continue proclaiming their heritage, i.e. by donning kilts . . . *plaide* is the Scottish Gaelic word—"

"Just as I thought," Rosco said.

Belle stared at him, dumbfounded. "You mean you were mulling over this very same subject at the very same time? Wow! I guess that's what marriage does for people. You start sharing thoughts as well as finishing each other's sentences."

"I suspect that we *weren't* sharing the same thought.

And when I said 'just as I thought,' I wasn't referring to acts of Parliament or Scottish kilts. I meant 'I thought' your mind wasn't focused on what I was saying, which it wasn't."

Belle continued to stare in perplexity. "Which was?"

Kit responded to this question with another stagy groan then stretched her long legs across the floor while Rosco answered an amused, "I asked if you planned on getting any shuteye tonight, or whether you intended to keep filling in empty white squares with your handy red pen."

Belle glanced at the photocopy of *"Holiday Slay Ride,"* the crossword recipe she'd been working on. "How can I sleep when I've got this conundrum in front of me?"

"Simple. You put down the book. Then you put down the pen. Then you climb the stairs, slide into bed, put your head on the pillow, and bingo: dreamland. Works for me every time. Unless, of course, you have a husband who insists upon being a pest."

"That's not what I mean, and you know it."

"At the risk of pointing out the obvious, this is an old cookbook you found at the inn, right?"

Belle cocked her head to one side. "And your point would be?"

"The mystery of who 'Mama' is—or was—as well as her daughter's identity has remained unsolved for a while. Maybe even a very long while. Another night's not going to make a difference. Dare I also suggest that given the somewhat lugubrious title these folks may even be deceased? Demised? Dead as a doornail? Six feet under? In which case you can get to it after the New Year. Valentine's Day, even."

"That's so callous, Rosco! Besides, I'm figuring the title is a clever turn of phrase for a 'killer' dessert. . . . Like a 'Death by Chocolate' kind of thing."

Rosco gave his wife a wry look. "Ask Gabby or Kit here if I'm the one who's being *callous*. . . . These are two seriously sleep-deprived pooches. Look at poor Kit; she's forced to lie on the *floor*, for Pete's sake. A hard, black and white floor."

Belle chuckled. "Well, you and your pampered pals can go back upstairs and snuggle under the quilt any time you wish. . . . Anyway, I'm almost finished." Her eyes returned to the puzzle, her pen poised in the air. "There are a number of references to movies and actors from the mid 1940s. . . ." she muttered, half to herself and half as an explanation to Rosco. "*Gorcey of* Mr. Wise Guy *and others,* which is the clue to 24-Across—the solution being *LEOS.* Then 42-Across: WALTER *Slezak of* Lifeboat; LENA *Horne of* Stormy Weather at 61-Across; *Bandleader Shaw,* which is obviously ARTIE at 2-Down. . . . If this puzzle was constructed later than the 1940s, there would be more contemporary clues."

By now Rosco had moved to Belle's side, and both dogs had given up on the humans, curling themselves into a disconsolate heap. The picture they created was one of both discomfort (the floor was chilly) and abandonment (the humans didn't love them sufficiently), but Belle and Rosco were familiar with these theatrical pleas for sympathy, and merely smiled at the supposedly woeful sight.

"You two sad sacks can head up to bed without us," Belle advised as she pointed her pen at 65-Across: *Miss Crawford's husband.* "See? The clue's in the present tense," she said to Rosco, "which means that the crossword must have been created when—"

"Well, it's not hubby *numero uno,* because Douglas Fairbanks, Jr. doesn't fit," Rosco interrupted. "And number two was Franchot Tone . . ."

Belle stared at her husband, slack-jawed with wonderment.

"Of course, Alfred Steele, the chairman of PepsiCo came way later . . . so the solution must be Phillip TERRY, the third spouse. I think the dates were '42 to '46 . . . Clark Gable was on the list, too, but not in the signed-on-the-dotted-line category. I believe their relationship was called a 'romance' back then, which remarkably brings us full-circle and back to that three letter word—B-E-D."

Belle finally found her voice. "How do you know bizarre facts like those?" she demanded.

"The same way you've picked up tidbits concerning the wearing of certain plaids."

Belle laughed again, then shook her head and regarded her husband with an amused expression. "You realize you look exactly like a fifties ad for pipe tobacco, don't you?"

Rosco also chortled. "I was afraid you'd say that. Just point me toward the brandy and the blazing yule logs. . . . Anyway, you're the one who gave me this sexy outfit, remember? Say, we don't have Prince Albert in the can, do we?"

Belle's smile grew. "Well, isn't it cozier than that threadbare black sweatshirt you're so fond of?"

But Rosco wouldn't concede this point. "Just remind me to change before I go into a waterfront dive pretending to be a disgruntled crew member who's lost his job on a fishing rig, and has a family of eight to feed. When I'm investigating a case of marine insurance fraud, that sweatshirt's a better choice than a dressing gown, plaid or otherwise . . . So, does *TERRY* fit?"

After Belle's chuckles subsided, she inked in the word. "Yup . . . but you haven't answered my question about why you know who Joan Crawford's various housemates were."

Rosco sidestepped the query with a breezy, "So that's the T at the end of PAT O'Brien, and the Y at the end of PENNY for *Singleton of* Blondie."

"Rosco," Belle protested. "Come on. Fess up. You're a secret Crawford groupie."

"Well, I'd like to say that as a PI who's done a fair

amount of divorce work, I've made it a habit to study nasty celebrity cases from the past as well as the present, but the truth is that my mom was a major Joan Crawford fan."

"You're kidding!" Belle couldn't imagine her mother-in-law, Helen, the quintessential Greek American matriarch—with the emphasis on Old World Greek—being a devoted admirer of filmdom's glamorpuss tough gal.

"Do I look as though I'm kidding?"

Belle gave her husband a knowing smile. "Yes, as a matter of fact. Just like you do a good deal of the time, I might add."

"So you thought I was joking when I suggested you and I could huddle under the sheets?"

Belle grinned, then tilted her face up to his, waiting for a kiss. "No, I know better than that."

"So we douse the lights, and—"

But Belle interrupted, almost jumping in her chair in her excitement. "Nineteen forty-two to '46. . . . Is that when you said this Phillip Terry was in the picture?"

"As it were—"

"Rosco! This is no time for puns!"

He gave her a mock frown. "I don't think I was the one who made the—"

But Belle was already on one of her proverbial tears. "*Lifeboat* was released in 1944. I know because I looked it up. John Steinbeck wrote the screenplay; bet you didn't know that one! Ditto on '44 for the Ameche flick *A Wing and A Prayer*. The other films were earlier. . . . Which means that this puzzle must have been constructed between '44 and '46."

"That sure narrows it down."

Belle ignored the facetious comment. "So, we have to find a mother whose daughter loved chocolate—"

"Will I sound like a broken record if I say, 'That sure narrows it down'?"

"Rosco—"

"And who may or may *not* have lived in Newcastle during the mid 1940s. Sounds simple enough. . . . Wait a minute, what's this 'we' business? How did *I* get involved in this?"

If Belle heard Rosco's question, she gave no indication that she had. "First thing tomorrow morning, I'm going to Legendary Chocolates. I'll bet they've got records dating back to the forties, and probably a whole lot earlier. The shop's been an institution in this city forever."

"I guess it wouldn't occur to you that this might be a wild goose chase," Rosco interjected.

"It's a chocolate chase," was Belle's blithe reply. "Geese, either wild or domesticated, have nothing to do with it. Although I imagine Legendary has all sorts of chocolate geese and turkeys made up for the holidays . . . and snowmen and snowflakes and elves . . ." She looked at her husband, her expression again thoughtful. "I wonder why it is that kids get such a kick out of biting the heads off chocolate creatures."

"As opposed to the pleasure adults feel doing the same thing?" Rosco chortled.

"Oh, I'm much more circumscribed when I devour a candy critter than I used to be."

"In that case, I'm glad I didn't know you way back when. I know better than to stand between you and your favorite foods."

"Ho, ho . . ." Belle rose and began turning off the lamps and shutting the puzzle-themed curtains against the cold night. Soon the room was reduced to basic black, with vibrant squares of white reflecting the lights still burning in the living room beyond. The sensation was akin to entering a three-dimensional word game.

She studied the scene while she reached out and took her husband's hand. "I bet you thought I was a nutcase when you first met me and saw where I did my best work."

"Actually, it was love at first sight," Rosco said as he embraced her. "The nutty part came later."

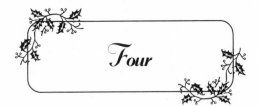

Four

AT seven-twenty the following morning, there was a light coating of snow covering the garden behind Belle and Rosco's house. It hadn't yet begun to stick to their narrow drive or the paved road that fronted the row of eighteenth-century houses that made up "Captain's Walk," but it soon would. The surprise snowfall was now predicted to continue all day, and perhaps into the night as well. At least ten inches was anticipated in the city, and more in the suburbs. Winter had officially arrived in Newcastle—or taken it by storm.

"Isn't it beautiful, Rosco?" Belle said as she sipped her coffee and stared through a kitchen window. She cupped her mug in both hands while she studied the scene. "Our first snow of the year. . . . Isn't it wonderful?" She sighed contentedly, then turned toward her husband. "Don't think for a minute, however, that it's going to delay my visit to Legendary Chocolates. No weather-wimp, am I."

"Mm hm . . ." Rosco helped himself to a second cup of coffee. Although he'd already taken his morning run accompanied by the two dogs, he wasn't necessarily fully conversant. Exercised, showered, shaved, and dressed, yes, but ready to have an intelligent dialogue, no. Belle, on the other hand, was primed for chat—just as she was every single morning. She actually woke up not only talking but often in mid sentence: the previous section of which had been left in her brain the night before.

"What time do you think the shop opens on Saturdays?" she asked with a cheery smile.

"Shop?" Rosco frowned in thought as he alternately stared at the coffee machine and his wife's sunny face.

"Legendary Chocolates . . ."

"Chocolate . . . ?"

At this point, Belle finally recognized that her mate wasn't yet equipped for this kind of speedy give-and-take. She chortled, walked to his side, and gave him a smooch. "Remember? Last night? My plan to start the search for our mystery crossword constructor at Legendary Chocolates?"

"Ah, the antique cookbook. . . ."

Belle chuckled again. "You're finally waking up.

Congratulations. It's a fine new day. And snowing, in case your hadn't noticed."

"Har har . . . The caffeine does begin to kick in eventually. Besides, I've already had my early morning encounter with the white stuff, remember?"

"What I don't understand, Rosco, is how you can go out jogging when you're still half in snoozeland."

"It's running, not jogging. And for all I know I'm moving my feet in my sleep. It's not an activity that requires a debating degree."

"Hmmm . . . The name for sleepwalking is somnambulism. What do you think sleep-running is? *Somniernan?*"

"What's 'iernan'?"

"Old English for *run.*"

Rosco shook his head. "I'm definitely going to need more coffee if you're insisting on yammering about etymology."

Belle raised a caustic eyebrow, then immediately jumped back to her earlier thought—a habitual activity that often made it difficult for her friends to keep up with her. "Well, let's see . . . my guess is that Saturday's a busy time in the confectionery world, and since Legendary prides itself on making its own products, someone in the family should be there by eight to crank up the machines or whatever they do, don't you think?"

Rosco knew better than to reply. Belle was fond of

posing questions she'd already answered. She glanced at the kitchen clock, an old-fashioned affair that needed winding every day and that seamlessly matched the retro appliances, the apple-green paint on the cabinets, and the dusty-rose linoleum floor: decor that had been in the house long before Belle and Rosco had come to inhabit it. "It's now seven thirty-four. . . . If I leave now, allowing a little extra time for slippery road conditions, I should be at Legendary by—"

"Aren't you forgetting something?" Rosco asked with an indulgent smile.

Belle forehead creased in thought. "The cookbook's in my purse . . . car keys, too . . ." She looked at her feet, which were already clad in the lace-up boots she used for inclement weather. "Well, my coat, obviously, but I'll grab that on my way out the door—"

"How about breakfast?"

"Breakfast?

"As in the stuff you eat first thing in the morning? The most important meal of the day, and all that?"

"Ah . . ." She gave him a wide grin. "I'm so accustomed to spending Saturday mornings with Sara and Al and the rest of the Breakfast Bunch down at Lawson's that I forgot everyone was decorating the inn and we needed to rustle up our own grub today."

"I don't believe you for a second," Rosco said, laughing. "You forgot about eating. Period."

"Okay, so I might have had a momentary lapse—"

"Right. And when was the *moment* you were going to remember that you'd gone without an entire meal?"

Belle also laughed. "This is why we make such a compatible couple, Rosco. While I'm fretting about cerebral curiosities, you're concentrating on life's basic requirements: food, shelter, getting enough shut-eye, wearing foul-weather gear if it's pouring . . . which is why I don't have to worry about any of those things. You do it for me. It's amazing how these things work out."

"Brawn versus brain, cereal versus cerebral, is that what you're saying?" Rosco asked as he pulled two bowls from a cabinet and filled them with granola.

Belle crossed behind him to open the refrigerator door and retrieve the yogurt they liked to spoon on top. As she passed her husband, she landed a quick peck on his cheek. "It's not an either/or situation, Rosco. . . . It's really brain *and* brawn. You get to do the physical bit because you're a he-man and cute." Then her brain made another rapid shift. "So what are you going to do while I'm on the trail of our elusive cook?"

"Oh, I thought I'd do some *shelter* activities: unclog all the drains, completely overhaul the furnace, fix any potential leaks in the roof, clean the gutters, maybe go out and shoot some bacon."

It took a moment before Belle realized he was joking.

"Seriously, what are you up to this morning? You finished your last case, right? So now what?"

"But not the support paperwork, and the final written report. Insurance companies are very fond of having all the *I*'s dotted and *T*'s crossed . . . so I guess I'll be forced to use my sluggish intellect."

"Very funny."

OLD Karl Liebig himself was at the cash register when Belle entered Legendary Chocolates. He was a short, frail man with thin white hair, a hearing aid, and an old world German formality. "Lee-bick" is how he pronounced his surname; the "Karl" was as guttural as a growl. Despite being a chocolate maker for over half a century, it was unusual to see him in a position of responsibility. A stroke, combined with age, had robbed him of a good deal of his memory; and his son, the current owner, generally provided his father with easier activities such as serving as a welcoming presence in the front of the shop. Karl Liebig might forget names or the year or any number of supposedly hard facts, but he still possessed a radiant smile and could produce a compliment for any age group and any occasion. He reminded Belle of one of Santa's most senior and jovial elves—albeit a slender one.

"Hi, Mr. Liebig," Belle called as she walked in. She

waved, as well, in case he'd heard the words but didn't immediately know who'd spoken them.

His response was a beatific beam. "Good afternoon," he said in the accent that proudly proclaimed his heritage. He gave Belle a courtly bow, bending from the waist like an antique mechanical doll. The gesture, combined with the stained-glass mural that filled the wall behind him, the shop's white marble countertops, and the curlicued, solid brass brackets that supported the shelves displaying the day's special wares, created a sense of elegance almost unknown in the twenty-first century food business. No shrink-wrapped, microwavable convenience goodies here. This was a place for discussion, consultation, and savoring possibilities. Should the caramels be covered with milk or dark chocolate? Would raspberry cream be preferable to butter-vanilla or nougat as a filling? Should the truffle have a mocha center or hazelnut or perhaps a hint of pistachio? Or what about hand-dipped fruit? Or cordial cherries spun in a chocolate skin? And that was just for starters.

There was also the aroma, which Belle considered wildly seductive. Why the men and women making and selling the sweets didn't each weigh four hundred pounds was anybody's guess. But there they were already bustling about: the three women and two men arranging the newest batch of treats in mouth-watering trays were not only *not* overweight, they seemed ageless; they could have been in their thirties or grandmothers of grandfathers of sixty plus. Maybe Legendary had discovered a new dietary fad.

"Good morning, Mr. Liebig," was Belle's warm but slightly embarrassed reply to his "Good afternoon." How did you respond to what was clearly a mistake without making the other person feel awkward?

She needn't have worried. Old Karl Liebig had already forgotten her and turned his concentration to the glass case that sat atop the central counter, repositioning a dish of hand-decorated peppermints as if he were rearranging a display of gemstones.

His son, "Young Karl," walked up the steps from the lower-level cooking and cooling rooms at that moment. Now nearing sixty, he'd been called Young Karl since the day he'd been born and doubtless would be long after his father was gone. This was Newcastle, after all, where memories outlasted one brief generation, and where patrons of the city's various businesses remembered visiting the city's shops with their own parents—or even their grandparents. If Stanley Hatch of Hatch's Hardware still found patrons who referred to him as "Old Mr. Hatch's grandson," then the current owner and manager of Legendary Chocolates didn't stand a chance of taking over his dad's name—at least for those in the fifty-and-up category. Belle, however, was in her thirties. To her, Mr. Liebig's son was simply Karl.

" 'Morning, Belle," he said. "I thought you'd be up at the inn with Sisters-in-Stitches. . . . I'm just finishing work on the chocolate village scene we're contributing to this year's holiday decor . . . dark, white, and milk: houses, people, and all. We even made molds of barns and buckboards and livestock. We can do that kind of thing fairly simply with polycarbonates. In my dad's time, we would have needed tin or steel. . . . The trees we're going to do in shortbread with cookie cutters and decorate them with greens sprinkles and white frosting for snow."

"I can smell the results," Belle said. "Or I can smell something fabulous. . . . Actually, I'm here because of a book I found yesterday. It's a cookbook, and it contains dessert recipes that are chocolate-based." She retrieved the slim volume from her purse. "Mitchell Marz couldn't remember where he'd found it, but I thought you might have records dating from the period, and that maybe—" Even as Belle said the words, she realized how foolish they sounded. A handwritten book by an anonymous author, circa 1944 to '46 and it wasn't even certain the other person came from Newcastle or even Massachusetts.

"And that maybe?" Karl prompted.

Belle's brow crinkled. "I know it's a long shot—a very long shot—but do your records list any of your clients' personal information: adults' or kids' birthdays or anniversaries—dates when they might have ordered something special? In other words, is there any way I might find a clue as to the person who created this volume? She dedicated it to her daughter, but the book hasn't been used. In fact, it seems almost like new, which leads me to wonder whether the daughter in question was a young child when her mother wrote these recipes for her . . . too young to know of the cookbook's existence."

Karl smiled; he had the same winning expression as his father, although in his case the smile had a wide-open Americanism instead of his dad's European decorum.

"Actually, what you're asking is a terrific question. We do keep those kind of personal records. And we pride ourselves on making sure they're up to date, sending out reminders about grandkids' birthdays—or greatgrandkids or parents or in-laws as the case may be, as well as special events. The files are computerized now, but I'm sure my dad kept previous lists. It would take me a while to turn them up, though, *if* I can, which is a big if. Dad has always been a bit of a pack rat; he had his own system of storing information. As you can imagine, it's not easy accessing it any longer."

Belle regarded the old man, who was now sunnily moving about the shop as if he had never had a care in the world.

As if he knew Belle was thinking about him, he turned toward her. "Would you care to see how we make chocolates here at Legendary?" he asked.

"Dad, Belle came here hoping to access some of our stored files," his son interjected, but the old man merely gazed at his offspring as though he wasn't certain they'd met before.

Then he began walking calmly toward the stairs that led down to the rooms where the candy was produced. "In my father's time, the molds for our holiday chocolates were often made of coin silver. Nowadays it's tin or steel. Not so pretty, but more economical. We do a handsome Kris Kringle just like my father remembers from the old country—two feet tall, in dark, milk, and white. White isn't technically chocolate, Miss, but cocoa butter, of course. We've found it's easier for customers to think of it as a color instead of a different substance. . . . And milk chocolate wasn't produced until 1875, which was only . . ." the old man paused, as though he'd lost his way through his journey through time, then his face suddenly brightened. "Ah! Our famous Kris Kringle. . . . As you can imagine, Miss, a mold as large as that formed out of silver would be prohibitively expensive."

"Dad. I'm not sure Belle has time for a tour," Karl interrupted, but his father ignored this suggestion as well.

"What did you say your name was, Miss?"

"Belle . . . Belle Graham."

Old Mr. Liebig laughed. "As in Alexander Graham Bell, or like jingle bell?"

Belle winced. As long as she could remember, her name had caused jests, but she didn't have time to respond, because Karl Liebig, Sr. was already marshaling her toward the stairs. "I only work in small batches, just like my grandfather did back in Germany before he emigrated to America. . . . Three generations of chocolate producers—which is a fine thing, isn't it? Small batches are the only way to maintain the appropriate temperatures for melting and tempering. Good tempering of the product is imperative if you want to avoid fat bloom. Besides, those big commercial kettles frighten me. I have a little boy, you know. Young Karl, named after me. Ever since that woman up Boston-way fell into a thousand-pound vat of melting chocolate and died, I've worried about my child. They didn't find the lady's body for two days. A grown person . . . and no one missed her. Well, I would miss my boy."

"What!" Belle gasped, but Mr. Liebig's momentary return to his younger days had passed, and he gazed at her uncomprehending then abruptly turned away from the stairs to take up a post near the shop's entrance instead.

"It's an old story of Dad's," Karl murmured. "It happened during the Second World War when women were hired for many of the jobs men had previously taken. Supposedly, she was doing maintenance repair on a catwalk above the vats and fell. I gather she wasn't on the regular payroll records, so no one missed her right off."

"How awful," Belle whispered. The image in her mind was not only ghoulish and gruesome, it was also horribly sad. A woman no one had missed. Hadn't she had family or friends who'd noticed she'd gone? Or could foul play have been involved?

But the questions were to remain unanswered, because a trio of customers walked into the shop at that moment, all scraping snow from their shoes and dusting off their coats as they stood in the doorway. "Looks like we're in for a heavier fall than they forecasted," one of them said with a good-natured groan. "Over a foot, maybe, they're saying now. The first snow of the year, and it's gotta be a doozy. I predict, folks, that we don't see the ground till springtime."

Old Mr. Liebig and his son both shook their heads in rueful acceptance of this hypothesis. Then Young Karl turned back to Belle. "I'll see if I can find Dad's old records. . . . What are those dates you wanted?"

"Nineteen forty-four to '46." As she supplied the information, Belle couldn't help but frown. The war years, she thought, when a woman had drowned in melting chocolate.

Five

WHILE Belle was in the midst of her unlikely quest at Legendary Chocolates, twelve-year-old E.T. Whitman was zipping up his parka, squashing his fleece-lined hat down on his head, and tugging on his boots and waterproof mittens. He considered even the fiercest blizzard to be an absolutely terrific part of life. Not because he enjoyed playing outside, although he most certainly loved sledding, building weird and scary alien snow creatures, ambushing unwary passersby with snowballs from behind a "fort" of hedges just like any other boy his age. No, the real reason E.T. was so crazy about the white stuff was because of his job shoveling the pathways at the Paul Revere Inn. And it wasn't just the money the Marz brothers paid him—although that was really, really nice—it was his sense of power and pride, which were two commodities in short supply in his home. At least, for him they were.

So as soon as the snow began to stick in earnest, accumulating in the crooks of the trees and coating the neighbors' fancy gardens, E.T. was dressed, out the front door, on his bike, and peddling down the hill. His agility with this two-wheeled vehicle would have been the envy of any downhill skier. As he caromed along on his mission, he often imagined that his home was still part of the large farm that had spread into the western wilderness back when Newcastle was still a whaling port—instead of what the house really was: a funny old clapboard building with a lot of fancier, newer homes nearby.

E.T.'s "response time" (he liked to set records for himself) was usually under fourteen minutes: what he referred to as "observation of snow accumulation to delivery of services." Zooming down the road, he considered how fortunate he was that it was a Saturday morning so he could spend all day at the inn, shoveling and reshoveling, putting out rock salt, deicing the steps. "Saturday A.M.," he corrected himself in an officious tone. "*Ante meridiem,* which is Latin for 'before noon.' P.M. is *post meridiem.* Who doesn't know that!"

He'd memorized a lot of similar facts, as well as other lesser-known but equally compelling expressions he found in the dictionary. The reference book was one of his all-time favorite reads (although this wasn't information he shared with anyone), and he perused it as avidly as he did tales of pirates or space monsters or people who could travel back and forth through time. The words he gleaned from a section entitled "Foreign Words and Phrases" came in handy when the other kids at school ganged up on him.

"Furor loquendi!" he'd yell at them, which translated to "rage for speaking," although he never revealed the truth. Or, *"Furor scribendi!"* which was "rage for writing." The kids who teased him guessed that the *furor* part had to do with fury, so they believed he was cursing them out or putting weird hexes on them. What dopes. But then they also made fun of his curly red hair. One particularly stupid classmate had even likened him to a troll. E.T. hadn't bothered to explain that the Vikings had the same wild red hair, and everyone knew you didn't mess with a Viking warrior. At least everyone living in the British Isles and Western Europe during the ninth and tenth centuries. After all, where did the word *berserk* come from if not from the Norse *berserksgangr*? But, again, that was information E.T. Whitman kept to himself. If his classmates had no desire to be illuminated, why bother?

He now squealed to a halt beside the inn's carriage, house that had been converted into a garage with an apartment above it for the chef. E.T.'s tires didn't actually make any sound in the new blanket of snow, but he supplied the noise himself: a sudden application of brakes, an out-of-control skidding across gravelly pavement, and a final, thudding crash. Sometimes he added a scream of alarm, or yelled, "Watch out below!" Today he had too much on his mind to create a big disaster.

Instead, he opened a side garage door that led into a square room that had once held the inn's saddles, horse blankets, bridles, and reins. Then he stepped around the mini-tractor used to cut the lawn, grabbed a snow shovel, and hurried toward the service entry to report for duty. The shovel was slung rifle-style over his shoulder, and he swaggered as he walked. He was small for a twelve-year-old, so the swagger took a certain amount of work.

The "M and M's"—E.T.'s private name for Morgan and Mitchell Marz—were not in the kitchen or pantry where he expected them to be. He wanted to check in with one of the twins personally, rather than simply telling the sometimes grouchy breakfast waitress, Joy Allman, that he was shoveling the walks, so he "parked his gear"—again his term—and hustled through the service doors into the guest area.

The age of the building never failed to stop E.T. in his tracks: the stone hearths where he imagined Revolutionary War soldiers filling their clay pipes and recounting that day's battle, the creak of the oak doorsills, the rattle of the ripply glass panes in the windows, the slanting stairs that certainly had ghosts still lingering on them.

"Mr. Mitchell," E.T. called out. "Mr. Morgan, I'm here to clear the paths." Curiously, no one was about. Although at 8:56 on a snowy Saturday morning in a place visitors chose because of its relaxing ambience, maybe only a twelve-year-old would find the lack of people strange.

"Mr. Mitchell? Mr. Morgan?" E.T. crossed the foyer and moved toward the front parlor where the famous poem sat enthroned in its big, elaborate frame. E.T. was certain he'd find one of the brothers there; it was where the morning newspapers were set out for the overnight guests.

"Then he said 'Good night!'," E.T. recited softly but dramatically. *"And with muffled oar, / Silently rowed to the Charlestown shore . . . "* He loved the "muffled oar" part, and he made hand and arm gestures indicating he was pulling hard on two invisible oar handles. *"A phantom ship, with each mast and spar, / Across the moon like a prison bar . . . "* Those lines always gave him goosebumps, which, of course, was the entire purpose in saying the poem aloud. Needless to say, E.T. had all thirteen verses of Longfellow's famous work memorized.

> *"Till in the silence around him he hears*
> *The muster of men at the barrack door,*
> *The sound of arms, and the tramp of feet,*
> *And the measured march of the Grenadiers . . ."*

E.T. entered the parlor. "Mr.—?" The words stopped in his throat as he looked at the desk and the wall above it. The poem was no longer proudly hanging there, and he could tell from the shattered glass ornaments that spread across the desktop and the greenery that lay trampled on the floor, that the picture frame had been grabbed a hurry. And there wasn't a newspaper in sight.

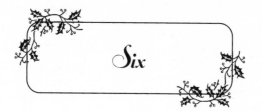

Six

ROSCO had just settled into his office chair and opened a hefty file folder to begin toiling away at his wrap-up of this latest insurance fraud case of his when the telephone rang—a welcome diversion, if truth be told. Anything that put paperwork on the back burner was just fine with Rosco. The call was from a near-frantic Mitchell Marz, informing him that someone had run off with the famous autographed Longfellow. Rosco knew the Marz brothers, of course; besides the Solstice Dinner and the awarding of the Holiday Decoration Competition prize, there were many pleasant meals he and his culinarily challenged wife had shared at the Revere Inn. But Mitchell spoke as if Rosco were not only a close family member, but as though the vanished poem had also been a cherished relative.

Naturally, Rosco's first bit of advice was to call the police. Mitchell told him that he and Morgan had already done so; someone from Robbery had arrived at the inn fifteen minutes earlier.

"Who'd they send?" Rosco asked. Out of habit he reached for a pad of paper and pen. Although he seldom read the directions for new electronics gadgets, and rarely relied on maps when driving to unknown locales, he did believe in writing down everything that pertained to business. The human brain had an uncanny facility for remembering misleading details.

"A Sergeant Fuller," the obviously shaken Mitch answered.

"Ohhh, boy," was Rosco's knowing response. Fuller had been with the Newcastle Police Department for nearly twenty-five years. When Rosco had worked for the NPD as a homicide detective, his path had crossed the Robbery Division, and Sergeant Fuller in particular, many times. Within the department, he was almost renowned for his slipshod work; and unless an honest pawn broker actually called to report a suspicious "fence" trying to unload something "hot," it was rare that the man ever solved a robbery or recovered anyone's lost property.

"I'll be right over," Rosco added, returning the phone to its cradle.

It took him a little over twenty minutes to work his way across town to the inn. The slick roads had already contributed to a few minor fender-benders, but Rosco's trusty Jeep, with its four-wheel drive, sailed through the salted slush and icy patches easily. When he walked through the inn's front door Mitchell was there to greet him. Behind him, several guests and a few members of the decorating clubs looked on in stunned silence. Sergeant Fuller was nowhere in sight.

"Fuller already left, I take it?" Rosco asked. He couldn't keep the sound of relief from his voice. The sergeant, like NPD's medical examiner, Herb Carlyle, were touchy when it came to criticism—either overt or not.

"No. He's in the kitchen having some breakfast."

Rosco instinctively glanced at his watch. "At ten thirty?"

Mitchell raised a single eyebrow. "I think it may be his second feeding—or third, judging by his girth. He doesn't seem to be taking much interest in the theft; that's why I decided to call you."

At that point Morgan appeared. His expression also displayed his concern over the vanished artwork, but he made a point of greeting the overnight guests and the returning decorators who'd braved the snow with a warm—if slightly forced—smile. "Sorry for this unfortunate disturbance, everyone. But if you make your way into the dining room, I can guarantee some dynamite chocolate-filled croissants our pastry cook just whipped out of the oven. . . . You know what they say about New England winters: extra weight's what gets you through the cold. . . . And if you're not partial to chocolate, we've got fresh cranberry bread and cinnamon buns . . ."

When the group had moved away, he and Mitchell led Rosco into the front parlor. "I was warning Mitch about this type of problem just yesterday," Morgan admitted with a beleaguered sigh. He stared at the wall where the Longfellow had been displayed. "This kind of situation isn't good for business. People worry about security when something like this happens—as well they should." He shook his head and looked bleakly at his brother, but Mitchell avoided the appeal. "I'd be less than honest, Rosco, if I didn't say that I disagreed with Mitch's decision to call you. So far, the police department has been very subtle in their approach, and that's just how I'd like to keep things. . . . How *we'd* like to keep things. Our patrons are here to escape the real world . . . not to have their faces rubbed in it. And the same goes for the decorating gang. Crime's not a fun diversion if you run a hotel and a popular restaurant."

"Oh, you can count on Sergeant Fuller on being subtle," Rosco responded with a thin smile. "Fuller's investigative techniques can out-subtle the best of them."

As if on cue, Fuller entered the room carrying a paper plate with six strips of bacon on it. He nibbled on a seventh, which he held in his right hand. After he finished it, he licked his fingers, wiped them on his trousers, and said, "Hey Polycrates . . . I thought you were out of business."

Rosco shrugged, appreciating the fact that Fuller hadn't extended his still-damp hand in greeting. "As long as NPD's Robbery Division works with its calculated efficiency," he said evenly, "there's no shortage of work for the private sector. . . . How's the bacon?"

"A little crispy for my liking." Fuller folded the paper plate around the remaining bacon strips. "Well my work here is done. I just stopped in to tell you gents that I'm off. I'll keep you posted on what I turn up."

"Aren't you planning to get someone in here to dust for fingerprints?" Rosco asked.

"This wasn't the *Mona Lisa,* Polycrates. Besides, it's my feeling that any prints walked right out the door with the picture frame." Fuller then turned and left.

"What a piece of work," Rosco muttered half under his breath.

"That's why I wanted to get you involved," was Mitchell's anxious reply. "Besides monetary value, there's the sentimental significance. The poem has been in our family for years; our guests remember it—even their kids and grandkids. It's one of our main attractions."

"Did Fuller do anything at all?" Rosco asked.

It was Morgan who responded. Despite his defense of the police department, and his stated unwillingness to call in a private investigator, he was clearly as troubled about the situation as his brother. "Basically, he just looked over our security system—or lack thereof—and then criticized it, suggesting that nineteenth-century locks can be easily picked, which, of course, is true. He also berated us for not having sensors on the windows or motion detectors." Morgan turned to his brother. "I told you we were walking on eggshells, here, Mitch. . . ."

"Well, hopefully the insurance will—"

"And what happens to our premiums, then, Mitch? Or our antiquated locks, or these wonderful old doors? Do you have any idea what the cost of upgrading—?"

"So the poem was insured?" Rosco interrupted.

Both men were silent for a moment. "Yes . . . ," Mitchell eventually offered, "for twelve thousand dollars."

Rosco let out a low whistle. "That's a nice chunk of change." He walked over and studied the wall where the poem had been hung. "It looks like it took a fair amount of effort to remove the frame. It was screwed in place, I gather?"

"Our father did that back in the 1940s; it hasn't been moved since," Mitchell told him. "You can see by the discoloration of the surrounding area that we've been painting around it for some time now."

"Did Fuller question any of the guests? Or the folks doing the decorating?"

"I don't want the guests questioned," Morgan said with some asperity. "Some are return customers and would feel insulted. Our first-timers would also. The same goes for the decorators—many of whom have been participating in the competition since its inception." Then he attempted a smile accompanied by a more jocular attitude. "I seriously doubt that Newcastle's most civic minded citizens are suddenly turning to lives of crime."

Rosco responded with his own small smile. "There's a chance that the very reason a customer—or a decorator—might *return* to the inn, Morgan, is because he or she saw something they liked and decided on a repeat visit in order to steal it. Whoever got your poem had to bring a screwdriver. Not an item I go on vacation with, but I'll bet your competitors had easy access to them." He glanced at his watch again. "Have any of your guests checked out since the poem went missing?"

"No," Morgan told him. "And none are scheduled to leave until Sunday."

"Who discovered the theft?"

"E.T.," Morgan said.

Rosco turned to face the two men. "E.T.?" The obvious reference to *extra-terrestrial* jumped to Rosco's mind, but he knew it wasn't the time for jests.

"He's a local boy who shovels our walks for us in winter, and cuts the grass in summer," Mitchell offered.

"Can I talk to him?"

"He's just a twelve-year-old kid," was Morgan's discouraged response. "What can he possibly tell you?" Then he again gazed pointedly at his brother. "Of all the weekends for this to happen . . . We've got most of Newcastle here, and a newspaper photographer due this afternoon. I told you no good would come of keeping all this valuable stuff on such prominent display, Mitch. Think of what this is going to do to our reputation." Then he walked from the room without bothering to wait for his brother's reply.

Rosco found E.T. sprinkling rock salt on the wooden steps that led to the inn's kitchen entrance. The boy was clearly impressed with Rosco's credentials.

"Wow, a private detective . . . That's way cool. The police have already been here."

"I know. Sergeant Fuller."

"Fuller? That's a good one. He sure was a lot *fuller* after he left. He spent more time in the kitchen than the parlor."

Rosco laughed. "I understand you were the first one on the scene?"

"Yep," he said proudly. "I reported it directly to M and M—that's Mitchell and Morgan; the Marz men; the Martians."

"That must have been pretty shocking news for them. How did they take it?"

E.T. folded his arms across his chest and gave Rosco a calculating laugh. "Yeah, I get it. . . . You're thinking the M and M's stole the poem themselves . . . for, like, the insurance money or something. And you want to know if they acted surprised when I told them it was gone. That's way, way cool." Then he thought for a second. "The problem is, I was the one who was upset. The M and M's both kept telling me to calm down. . . . I guess I got a little hyper. I do that sometimes. . . . I mean, Mr. Mitchell was nice about it, but Mr. Morgan . . . well, I don't think he likes me very much."

"I take it you didn't see anyone walk out with the artwork, or act suspicious in any way?"

"Nah. None of the guests took it, that's for sure."

"You sound awfully certain."

E.T.'s face assumed a serious and adult expression. He pointed to a small parking area. "See those cars over there? They belong to the overnight guests. No footprints in the snow. No one's opened a trunk or car door." He then pointed to the another lot. "Now, those vehicles belong to the people who came in this morning to do the decorating. Look at all the footprints. I think we should get them all to open their trunks. I'll bet that's who stole it; one of them, anyway."

Realizing the twelve-year-old could be a good ally, Rosco said, "I like that theory, E.T.; you're very observant. But you know, a guest could have just taken the frame straight to a bedroom. An employee living in the building could have done the same thing. *Or,* our culprit could have been someone who snuck in during the middle of the night and left long before you came to work."

"Culprit," E.T. echoed. He appeared to enjoy the sound of the word. "Is that from, like, culpable?"

Rosco chuckled. "You'd have to ask my wife. She's the crossword editor of the *Crier*, and she spends her days parsing language."

E.T.'s eyes grew huge. He looked not only delighted but also awe-stricken, as if Rosco had just mentioned he were married to a famous actress or pop star. "You mean, Belle Graham? That's your wife?"

"None other."

"Way cool . . ." Then E.T. grew suddenly shy, which he masked by standing straighter and returning to the subject of the missing poem and his own role of self-appointed investigator. "Well, we can't make everyone open the trunks of their cars, because Mr. Morgan doesn't want to make a big stink."

Rosco nodded. "No . . . I have to go on the premise that it's already left the property. The sooner I can get autograph dealers apprised of the theft, the harder it will be to sell it. But I'm going to need someone to keep an eye out for suspicious behavior here at the inn."

E.T. puffed out his chest. "I'm your man, Mr. Poly-crates."

Rosco handed him a business card and winked. "Call me Rosco."

Reading the card, E.T.'s face grew serious. "I guess you chose your alias because roscoe's slang for a gun. . . .

How come you didn't call yourself Rosco Sten . . . or Gat . . . or Barker? Those words mean gun, too."

E.T., Rosco realized, was going to make a good match for Belle one day. "I'll give it some thought . . . but for now, let's keep our eyes peeled for a *culpable culprit*."

Seven

THE storefront of the Olde Print Shoppe in downtown Newcastle was as picturesque as any tourist could wish: an old-fashioned floor-to-ceiling bay window bisected by mullions painted a glossy black. In summer, a dark awning and pots of red and pink geraniums completed the pleasing scene, but in the middle of a new snowfall, the enterprise looked almost too cinematic to be real: wisps of dazzling white drifting along the shiny panes, or, like frosting, lapping the base of the building and curling up the front steps—while the interior cast out a warm, pink light beckoning passersby to stop in for a relaxing perusal of its handsome and pricey artwork.

As Rosco parked his Jeep and crossed the street, he

almost believed he'd spot stagehands and a snow-making machine, or actors awaiting their cues while clad in Victorian cloaks; the men tipping tall glossy hats to the ladies in snow-dusted bonnets. The red Jeep, he decided, was a definite anomaly; a horse and carriage would have better fit the bill.

He entered the shop and was greeted by the owner herself, a tall, broad-shouldered, exuberant woman with a booming voice, as well as a scattered manner that didn't match her physical presence. Her French-English name mirrored the duality of her nature: Coco Barre; and she was well-known for being both a romantic idealist and an exacting businesswoman. If she didn't consider a client worthy of a piece of art, she wouldn't sell it no matter how much money was offered. However, those collectors who met with her approval could run up large tabs without fear of being cut off. What was all-important to Coco Barre was that the prints and drawings and manuscripts in her shop found appropriate homes.

"Welcome! Welcome!" she called out, pushing strands of graying hair back into what was obviously a lopsided bun. The hair escaped; she shoved it into place again, and again lost the fight. "Are you looking for a gift? Or might you be here to choose something for yourself? I have a very handsome Charles-Lucien Bonaparte folio that just arrived only this week. It includes fifty-five hand-colored lithographed plates devoted to various species of pigeon." Clearly Rosco had passed her acid-test on looks alone. Despite her age, she hadn't lost an eye for members of the opposite sex.

"Pigeons?" Rosco asked. All he could imagine were the annoying gray variety that made a mess of city streets and park benches and statues.

"No, I see I'm mistaken about the Bonaparte, exceptional as it is. You're not a bird enthusiast. . . . In fact, on second glance, you look like a collector of maritime works. Would a two-color lithograph concerning whale hunting be of interest? It's a highly dramatic scene entitled *The Capture* and was published in 1862. It would make a very attractive addition to any office decor, but I would suggest a discreet frame so as not to detract from the bold vitality of the work, itself. . . . If not *The Capture,* I have many other nautical and marine—"

"Actually," Rosco interrupted before the gallery owner could roll out additional examples of pictures he couldn't afford, "I'm here to solicit your expert opinion. Some say you're the best in the business."

Coco Barre smiled, obviously flattered. Instead of turning coquettish as some women might, she seemed to grow in stature until she almost towered over Rosco. "Yes?"

Rosco produced his business card, and she read it in silence. "Has something been stolen, Mr. Polycrates?" she asked. The dreamy side of her personality was nowhere in evidence; the woman was wholly professional now.

Normally, Rosco would have questioned this quick assumption, wondering if the person he was interviewing had prior knowledge about the case, but the owner of the Olde Print Shoppe seemed far too forthright to be able to lie successfully. "The inn's signed copy of Longfellow's *Paul Revere's Ride.*"

"Oh, my goodness," was her stunned reply, and her expression replicated the perplexed and astonished faces Rosco had encountered when he'd interviewed Mitchell and Morgan: a robbery at such a well-beloved spot couldn't—and shouldn't—happen. "But the Longfellow's been hanging in that front parlor for decades. . . . The Marz twins' grandparents renamed the inn for the poem when they purchased the property during the twenties."

"So it must be pretty valuable?" Rosco prompted.

Coco frowned in thought as she fiddled ineffectually with her recalcitrant hair. "Valuable enough, surely, but hardly worth stealing. . . . Well, no, that's not quite true. A theft can be for monetary gain; it can also be inspired by covetousness. Famous paintings go missing from museums on a regular basis. A case in point is *The Scream* by Edvard Munch, an incredibly well-known image that would likely bring seventy million dollars at auction. It was swiped in broad daylight in Norway and joined the list of over one hundred fifty thousand missing treasures: Picassos, Rembrandts, van Goghs, Renoirs, to mention some of the biggies. What happens to the pieces? Obviously, a criminal reaps a reward, but so does the collector who purchased it on the black market. . . . But then he or she must keep the object secret. It's not my idea of displaying favorite artwork—where only one selfish person can gaze upon it. . . . There's also the issue of theft for ransom . . . a form of extortion, really. I'm afraid the darker side of the art world is far more sinister than people imagine."

Rosco considered this information as he made notes of what she'd said. "What do you mean by 'valuable enough,' Ms. Barre?"

"I'm ashamed to say I haven't given the poem more than a cursory glance for some time, so I can't attest to what kind of shape the paper's in, how well the signature has survived, if there's light damage, etc. . . . There certainly has been a lot of traffic through that room over the years; and as I recall the parlor was designed as a gentlemen's smoking area up until the 1960s, which doesn't make for an ideal climate. Who knows how well the display was sealed, and so forth . . . ? But I can tell you that we're not talking about a framed manuscript. For instance, I have a poem here by A.A. Milne, handwritten and signed, that sells for ten thousand dollars. Milne's English, of course; Longfellow's quintessentially American, but both authors have achieved a kind of cult status. If the print at the inn had been a hand-penned manuscript, it would be worth a good deal of money." Her frown deepened. "I'm sure Mitchell Marz would have had the piece insured with other fine arts at the inn; the policy would require an appraisal performed by someone certified in the field."

Rosco nodded. "Obviously, you didn't appraise it."

"Despite the antiquarian look of this shop, I'm not as old as that, Mr. Polycrates. The Longfellow poem was purchased by the Marz twins' grandparents long before I arrived in the world." Coco laughed. Then she again grew serious. "So . . . if the monetary value is fairly simple to assess—which it should be once you factor in the date of the last appraisal, add for inflation and shifts in market appeal, etc.—"

"The Marz brothers have it insured for twelve thousand dollars."

Coco Barre looked astonished. "That amount seems extraordinarily high. Admittedly, I haven't seen the piece in quite a while, but twelve grand . . . Wow . . ." She shook her head. "If the Marz twins don't have a bona fide appraisal by a legit house, their insurer isn't likely to pay off on some fictional figure. As a PI, I'm sure you've had numerous dealings concerning fraudulent or inflated claims."

Rosco could only nod as he remembered the paperwork from his last case sitting abandoned on his desk. "I believe Mitchell Marz is more concerned with recovery than insurance money."

"So you say. Be careful; art thieves are better actors than anybody on Broadway. But what you're here to ask me is how a thief unloads the goods, correct? And do I know a likely *fence?*"

Rosco smiled. There was something very appealing in a person who could rattle off details about the art world as well as talk in common vernacular. "I'd appreciate whatever insight you can provide, Ms. Barre."

"Well, obviously, no one's going to be stupid enough to bring it here, Mr. Polycrates, and Boston's proximity makes it equally off-limits. Then again, given the Internet and how quickly dealers in any type of antique receive word about stolen objects, I'm not sure where any criminal takes hot material anymore. Those Rembrandts and so forth I just mentioned didn't simply vanish into a black hole . . . which brings me back to a type of insider situation. Someone wanted that particular print . . . either a Longfellow aficionado or a history buff. I doubt it would be simply collector of autographs or manuscripts. There are too many other sources to tap. My hunch is that you've got semi-kook on your hands. Someone who was willing to remove a large and highly visible item—and from a place that's got a lot of traffic, albeit not much security—and then hide it away like a squirrel burying a nut."

"A nut with a nut . . ."

"I'm sorry I didn't think of that line first, Mr. Polycrates."

Eight

UAL pyramids fashioned from sacks of rock salt stood beside two weathered wooden barrels containing shiny, new snow shovels: a winter-is-really-here display that welcomed patrons to Hatch's Hardware Store. Behind this salt-and-shovel extravaganza, the shop windows bracketing the door were cluttered with forty-pound sacks of bird seed, gallon containers of lamp oil, antifreeze, windshield deicer, and the occasional boxed and beribboned chain saw, electric drill, or work boots. It was a vintage Martha Stewart–type moment for those who believed that household improvement was a matter of penny nails, claw hammers, and galvanized deck screws; and the place was bustling with the good cheer that accompanied any change of weather. Autumn's leaves had been raked and bagged—or burned, for those could get away with it. Now it was time for snowplows, extra weight in the truck bed for traction, and emergency tire chains: all the elements of wholesome New England living.

Another sign of the season was a large wooden barrel that sat just inside the entryway, a repository for holiday toys, games, books, fuzzy creatures, and dolls that were collected each year by Newcastle's merchants for children who were less fortunate than others. Rosco was part of the team that wrapped and distributed the gifts, although that wasn't what had brought him here today. Not that he didn't have plenty of excuses for why he absolutely, positively needed to stop by Hatch's. For one thing, conversation was always lively—more so during heated political contests, which thankfully had become ancient history by Thanksgiving—and old friends were bound to be there just to talk. Plus, there was all that neat stuff. Not that Rosco had any idea how to use an electric planer or joiner or router, but it sure looked as if he should own one just in case the need arose.

But on this particular Saturday, it was E.T. who had influenced his decision. *Rock salt,* Rosco had thought, *surely we'll be needing more rock salt.*

As he joined the line of customers standing alongside the counter waiting to pay for their various supplies and home-repair gizmos, he lifted a screwdriver from a display box and studied it. This particular tool could be converted for use with flat-head or Phillips-head screws by simply changing the tips neatly stored in a removable handle. It was a nifty item, compact and discreet; and Rosco was in the midst of examining it when Al Lever, Newcastle's chief homicide detective, approached from behind.

"It's a screwdriver, Poly—Crates," he said facetiously. Al's exaggerated and butchered pronunciation of Rosco's last name had been a part of his lexicon since the two had been joined up as partners in the NPD more than fifteen years prior. Their friendship had continued long after Rosco had left the department: Lever, in his forties, balding, often irascible, forever losing his battle with a weight problem, and plagued by an eternal smoker's cough, versus the athletic and even-tempered Rosco. No wonder the jibes flew fast and furiously. "A screwdriver, buddy-boy; it's used by those dexterous folks in the auto repair and carpentry trades for setting, or removing, screws. Would you like me to show you how one works?"

Rosco laughed. "No, no, I'm going to figure this one out on my own, Big Al. Screwdriver, huh? Well, I'll be . . . I thought that had something to do with orange juice?" He then extended his hand to Lever. "Day off, I take it?"

"Even public servants get one every now and then."

An ancient collie by the name of Ace, companion to the store's owner, Stanley, and a permanent fixture at

Hatch's, ambled up, sat beside Rosco, and leaned his weight against Rosco's leg. Rosco reached down and gave him an affectionate pat. "Sorry, Ace old man, neither Gabby or Kit are with me today. They're kind of weather-wimps; curled up on heated beds at home."

"It's a dog, Poly-crates, not a person. I wouldn't put too much stock in Ace's ability to comprehend compound sentences."

Rosco gave Al a sideways glance. "So I gather your pal, Skippy, is the only dog in Newcastle that understands human speech?"

"Yeah . . . well . . . Skippy's a different story," Lever blustered. "See, a stray like The Skipper needed to gauge people's lingo in order to survive. It's remarkable how bright he is."

"For a dog . . ."

"Well . . . yeah."

"I see. And I assume Skippy shared all this information with you—which is why you're so free and easy with the compound sentences while yakking with him in the park."

Lever seemed to have no response to this statement. Ace's reaction to the exchange was to stand and head toward the rear of the store, walking heavily across Lever's shoes as he passed.

"I think that beast's going blind," Lever groused as he tried to move his feet out of the way.

"Don't count on it," Rosco laughed.

"Anyway, Poly—Crates, Buck Fuller tells me you've been brought in by the Marz brothers."

"Yep. Confidence in the good Sergeant Fuller seems to be low at the Paul Revere Inn. I don't suppose any interesting theories or tidbits have popped up over at NPD?"

Lever raised his beefy arms. "Please, don't get me involved with more work than I need. I'm Homicide, remember? If someone turns up dead, give me a call. Otherwise I don't want to know from nothin'."

"What brings you two out on this snowy morning?" Stanley Hatch asked as approached, giving Lever a friendly thwack on his back and shaking Rosco's hand.

"Rock salt," Al and Rosco answered in unison, and also laughed as a team. Then Lever pointed to the doorway. "Well, well, here comes *Mr. Casanova,* the Good Doctor Jones . . . Since his condo's on the eleventh floor, I'd venture to say he's *not* here for salt."

Abe Jones was the Newcastle Police Department's chief forensics expert; a tall, exceptionally good-looking African American who'd been more than instrumental in helping both Al and Rosco solve a plethora of crimes. He approached the three men and all exchanged greetings.

"We're taking bet's here, Abe," Stanley said with a smile, "on what brings you into Hatch's Hardware today."

"Rock salt."

This brought on another round of laughter, followed by a lengthy coughing fit by Al. "Dang allergies follow me year round," he wheezed.

"Dang Camels follow you year round, is more like it," Abe jested. "You oughta start your own desert caravan. . . . It's never too late to quit, you know?"

"Yeah, yeah, thank you for the advice *Doctor* Jones. It's nothing I haven't heard before. . . . And what's with you and the rock salt? Maintenance guys at your spiffy condo on strike?"

"No. I was with this new lady-friend of mine last night. She just bought a house near yours, Rosco. . . . Anyway, you guys know how it is; next thing you know they've got you roped into doing the domestic thing."

Lever again raised his hands. "Please, spare us the gory details of your love life, Don Juan."

Abe glanced at his watch. "Well, I'd sure like to hang around and gab, but I've got to scoot." He poked Al in the belly and winked. "See, we weren't quite finished up with what we got started last night, if you know what I mean."

He stepped around the others, paid for his rock salt, and grabbed a sack on his way out the door.

"Who knew the way to a woman's heart was through a sack of salt?" Stanley mused. "Welcome to Massachusetts, I guess."

"I suspect that my wife won't be moved to any lustful fantasies when she sees me walk in with the stuff."

"One never knows, Al. Maybe you should buy two sacks; make an evening of it," Stanley chortled. "Not to change the subject, but that's a real shame about the poem being stolen. Martha phoned me about it a little while ago. Any leads, Rosco?"

Rosco shook his head. "Not a one."

"Well, old man Marz couldn't have paid too much for it back in the twenties, or whenever the heck it was," Stan continued. "At least, that's what my dad said. Not that it wasn't a really nice addition to the place—whatever the price."

"So your father knew the family?" Rosco asked.

"Oh, yeah, the old man and his son, Mike, too. They were all members of the same VFW post. It was old Milton who bought that poem and decided to change the name of the inn. He died in the late thirties, if I remember correctly. A genuine kook, according to my dad. . . . Kept the place just like it was when he bought it, insisted folks wanted authenticity in a historic building: no electricity, only candles and oil or gas lamps, gas stoves, working fireplaces. It wasn't wired for juice until Mike—that's the twins' father—took over the business. And then when Pearl Harbor was bombed, and he enlisted in the Army and left his wife to run the show. The twins must have been pretty young then. Probably wasn't easy on her, either, keeping the old place going with two little kids and all. Plus worrying about the hubby."

"Uh . . . huh," Lever nodded in thought as he reached for a cigarette.

"Sorry, Al, can't smoke in here."

"Come on, it's a hardware store, Stan. Smoking's part of the . . . tradition. Mano-a-mano. Cigars. Pipes—"

"Not in the twenty-first century, it isn't."

Al begrudgingly slipped his Camels back into his shirt and Rosco said, "The twins' father died pretty soon after returning from the war, didn't he?"

"Yep. Something tells me it was around 1948, or maybe 1949? Just before I arrived on the scene, anyway. . . . It was a hunting accident; Mike was accidentally shot by another hunter. I remember my dad saying what a shock the whole thing was for the community." Stan shook his head, reminiscing. "Newcastle was a smaller place back then; everybody cared about everyone else. . . ." Then Stanley Hatch's expression changed, turning into a quiet, reflective smile. "Another thing my dad told me was that the guys at the post loved to tease Mike Marz about screwing old Henry Wadsworth Longfellow to the parlor wall—like someone was going to steal him. . . . Apparently, Mike didn't appreciate all the ribbing."

Rosco placed the screwdriver back in the display box and said, "Yeah, well, I guess now the joke's on us."

Angel in Disguise

Sift together: ¾ cup flour; ¾ cup *30-Across* sugar; ¼ cup cocoa

Combine and beat until soft mounds appear: 1½ cups *46-Across;* 1½ tsp. *25-Across;* ½ tsp. salt; 1½ tsp. *18-Across*

Beat in until stiff: ¾ cup additional *30-Across* sugar, 2 tbsp. at a time

Sift in dry ingredients; then fold in: 1 cup *51-Across*

Gently pour batter into 10 inch ungreased *63-Across*

Bake at 325 degrees for 50 minutes

This will serve 14, if your guests aren't greedy . . .

ACROSS

1. Comic's bit
4. Place to wipe your feet
7. Manuscript modifiers; abbr.
10. Playwright's monogram
13. Three-match link
14. Eggs; in biology
15. Certain mushroom
16. Knock on the door
17. Giant baseball player?
18. MAMA's DESSERT
20. Lengthen
21. Electron tube
23. Bug
24. Beef & potato dish
25. MAMA's DESSERT
28. Caesar's 102
29. The Caribbean is one
30. MAMA's DESSERT
36. Ordinance
40. Too much in France
41. Facade
43. _____ Cruz
44. Miss Loos
46. MAMA's DESSERT
48. French pronoun
50. Sup
51. MAMA's DESSERT
58. Jaw
59. Surly
60. Movie light
62. Erase
63. MAMA's DESSERT
65. _____ Magnon
66. Pub pint
67. Here in Paris
68. Employ

69. Argentine president Juan's wife
70. Drs.
71. Born
72. Salary
73. Bro or sis

DOWN

1. Fine
2. Prank
3. Crock's cousin
4. Fan's job?
5. Mickey's wife of a year
6. Latin-American dance
7. Acclaim
8. River basins
9. Retreat
10. Miss Garbo
11. Cake maker
12. Gush
19. Eternity; abbr.
22. Trick
24. Remain active
26. Petty quarrel
27. Yank's foe
30. RR stop
31. Coffee server
32. Hawaiian staple
33. Anger
34. Holiday quaff
35. H.S. subj.
37. Allow
38. "These _____ the times . . ."
39. Had been
42. Dainty
45. Matterhorn; e.g.
47. Hired coach
49. Fir kin

🌴 *Angel in Disguise* 🌴

51. Tot
52. Pelts
53. James Hubert Blake, familiarly
54. A general monogram?
55. Rejuvenate
56. Better
57. Tennis shot

58. Study & study
61. Hockey score
63. Can material
64. Thin-rail link

Nine

LAWSON'S Coffee Shop didn't seem like Lawson's without Martha Leonetti there to sass her favorite customers. Oh, the bright pink vinyl banquettes were the same, as were the coral-colored formica tabletops, the other waitresses' rose-hued uniforms, the chrome fixtures behind the counter, the chrome napkin dispensers arranged neatly upon it, and the chrome and leatherette swiveling stools, but a definite vitality was lacking. And not even the robust voice of Kenny, the fry cook—or "King Kenny," as Martha liked to call him—could make up for her absence.

Hunched over a copy of the "Angel in Disguise" crossword recipe that was spread before her, Belle surveyed the scene. "I don't like this, Rosco," she said.

"What? The coffee's no good because Miss Wisenheimer didn't pour it? Or do you mean the grilled cheese, which you've hardly touched because you're too busy filling in small white squares with a red ballpoint pen?"

Belle's response was to gaze past her husband, staring at the windows and the snow that was now tumbling from the skies in earnest. Outside, the world appeared to be vanishing under this weight of white. "No," she admitted. "I don't like having Martha up at the inn instead of here. I missed our Breakfast Bunch gathering this morning, missed Sara and Al—and you—trading quips and laughter. . . . I guess I'm just a person of habit."

Rosco took her hand. "Speaking of habits . . . I wish you'd remember that if you say you're going to beam in with me via cell phone, you're supposed to do it."

"You don't need to worry about me, Rosco. I'm a good driver."

"I realize that, but you worry when I'm doing something you consider unsafe, don't you?"

Belle sidestepped the question by returning to the puzzle. The recipe was the real deal, an old-fashioned chocolate-pecan angel food cake created by a genuine cook. "69-Across: *Argentine president Juan's wife,*" she muttered. "5-Down: *Mickey's wife of a year* . . . 53-Down: *James Hubert Blake, familiarly.* You really need to know your history to keep up with this gal. . . ." Even as Belle spoke, she wrote in EVA, AVA, and EUBIE.

Rosco gazed at her and chuckled. "I'm looking forward to having you meet E.T. Whitman. He seems as much of a word freak as you are. And, boy, was he ever impressed when I told him I was your husband."

"Happy to oblige." Belle grinned, then picked up her sandwich. "Who would name a kid E.T.? It's like Ima Hogg."

"Yeah . . . I bet he doesn't have an easy time of it at school. I'm sorry to say that Morgan Marz seems kind of hard on him, too."

Belle continued to eat, swishing her French fries in a puddle of ketchup. "Morgan's not always easy on Mitch, either. . . . So, what's your take on the disappeared Longfellow?"

"Listen, my children, and you shall hear, Of the midnight ride of Paul Revere," Rosco quoted dramatically. *"On the eighteenth of April, in Seventy-five . . ."*

Belle chuckled, continuing the stanza in her own theatric tone. *"Hardly a man is still alive—"* Then her words abruptly ceased and her eyes grew wide and worried. "Wouldn't it be awful if this cookbook were connected to the woman who drowned in the chocolate vat? The one old Mr. Liebig remembered."

Rosco shook his head. "I'd say that was a long shot. You told me the woman was working on the catwalk above—"

"Cleaning machinery," Belle interjected.

"Exactly, cleaning," Rosco continued. "I don't want to seem snooty, but someone hired for that type of job . . . well, let's just say that the members of my family who first arrived in this country grabbed any kind of work they could. It was always menial. . . . No slur intended, but they weren't crossword constructors."

"I hear what you're saying, Rosco. I know creating puzzles requires a certain level of education, not to mention a command of the English language . . . but when that woman died, we were at war. I'll bet a lot of literate people took work that might have been beneath them just to make ends meet when their loved ones were far away fighting. And besides, maybe she didn't fall. Maybe she was pushed. A love triangle situation, or—"

The arrival of Stanley Hatch curtailed the rest of Belle's hypothetical scenario. "Mind if I join you two?"

Rosco and Belle immediately slid over to make room. From the focused manner in which Belle studied Stan, Rosco sensed she was about to bring up the subject of Martha. He nudged his wife's foot under the table. It was one thing for Sara to act as matchmaker; women her age were entitled to meddle. Belle, however, was nearly a half century younger.

Belle's reaction to this warning was to raise her eyebrows in an exaggeration of innocent denial.

"I need some advice," Stan stated somberly. "It's about Martha."

Belle shot her husband a triumphant glance, then graced Stan with her sweetest and most naive expression. "What about Martha?"

"Well, you know we ended up being Secret Santas last year . . ."

Which was totally manipulated by Sara, Belle thought but didn't say.

"And we've been sort of . . . well, you know, spending time with each other now and again since then, and—"

"You mean dating," Belle tossed in with another syrupy smile, and Rosco poked her foot again.

"Well, yeah . . . I guess . . . sure . . . 'dating' . . ." Stan looked so tenuous that he reminded Belle of a young deer who'd been caught in the headlights without the reassuring presence of mom nearby. Then she decided, no: *A fawn would have more self-assurance.*

"And, well . . . ," Stan continued, ". . . what I want to know is: Would it be appropriate for me to get her a gift this year? No Secret Santa. Just me to her. And something personal, like a pretty piece of clothing or well . . . something."

"Why not?" Belle asked brightly.

"Yeah," Rosco added, "It's not like anybody's *watching* or anything." This time Belle kicked him under the table.

Stanley scowled self-consciously, his tall body bending over the table. "I don't want to put pressure her. I mean, you know how vivacious Martha is . . . always coming up with the snappy retorts, the life of the party, and all that; and I'm just, well, I'm just me, owner of a

Mr. Fix-it shop, which isn't exactly a sexy business. . . . She called me today—from the inn—but it was just to report the theft."

I'll just bet that was the reason! Belle told herself, but again didn't reveal what she was thinking.

"There's nothing wrong with owning a hardware store, Stan," Rosco insisted. "It's my very favorite place in the city. . . . But yeah, like you said, it's not all that romantic as a profession, but—"

Belle jabbed her husband's ankle with her toes again, halting this incredibly inappropriate mini-monolog, and finishing it with her own more suitable words. "But . . . but Martha loves the shop," she announced.

"Really?" Stanley looked at Belle in wonderment. "She told you that?"

Belle gazed calmly back, avoiding Rosco's surprised stare altogether. "Rosco and I are all thumbs when it comes to home-improvement paraphernalia," she all but cooed. "And so is Martha. That's why she loves Hatch's. It's like . . . it's like . . . seeing a big Broadway musical for the first time—watching all those fabulous sets moving around, and people singing and dancing and dropping from the skies. . . . It's so astonishing and de-lightful; you just don't know where to look next."

Rosco decided that the pragmatic Stanley was going to start guffawing at Belle's over-the-top analogy, but Rosco was wrong. Stan bought it hook, line, and sinker. "Really?" he repeated with genuine pride.

"And all those beer-bellied stagehands pounding nails into broken scenery, not to mention long-legged dancers in net stockings." Rosco added, but Stan was too far gone for the joke.

"So you're telling me it's okay if I buy Martha a real gift?" he asked Belle in a hushed but thrilled tone.

"I think she'd be horribly disappointed if you didn't, Stanley," was Belle airy reply. "Just horribly." Then she added an equally breezy "In fact, I'd love to help you pick out that perfect token of your friendship." Belle deliberately moved her foot in order to avoid Rosco's next warning nudge. "I've got something really special in mind."

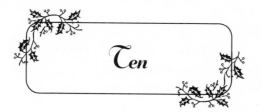

Ten

IT was E.T. who ran up to Rosco and Belle as they stepped out of the Jeep. The twelve-year-old's excited rush of words were aimed at Rosco, but his focus was wholly on Belle. "Mr. Morgan's gone to Boston," he stage-whispered in his best junior-spy voice, "which is really, really suspicious. Why would anyone go up there in all this snow? I bet he's got the poem and is going to fence it! In fact, how do we know he's really going to *Boston?* That's only hearsay." As if he'd just remembered his manners, he whipped off his hat and stuck out his hand, adding a self-important, "I'm E.T. Whitman. Your husband asked me to keep an eye on things."

"Belle, I'd like you to meet another language aficionado," Rosco said with a broad smile.

E.T. seemed to grow an inch or two, and his flaming red hair all but quivered with pride. "But if Mr. Morgan did go up there, it must have been for something totally nefarious."

Belle grinned as she shook E.T.'s hand. *Nefarious* was one of her favorite words, too. "I've heard a lot about you, E.T. Thanks for helping." She didn't have the heart to tell him that Mitchell had already explained that his brother had had a long-standing commitment to attend the city's traditional and contemporary furniture exposition, but Rosco knew he needed to set the record straight.

"Mr. Morgan's considering purchasing some new furnishings for the inn," he said. "That's why he drove to Boston today. He had an appointment with a design consultant. He's due back tonight. Mr. Mitchell told us all about it."

The term *crestfallen* might have been invented for E.T.'s reaction to this news. His head and shoulders sagged; his smile drooped; even his springy hair looked deflated and flat. "Oh . . ." He looked at his feet. "Yeah . . . Mr. Morgan's always saying there's too much old stuff around . . ." Then E.T. seemed to recover a little of his feisty spirit. "We've had four and a half inches of snow since you left, Rosco, which makes almost seven. I measured it. None of the cars in the overnight lot have been moved or visited, and no one's carried anything into or out of the inn. That goes for the decorators, too, although they've all gone home on account of the weather. I've been watching everyone, and I can promise you nobody had the poem." He paused and scowled in concentration. "Okay, here's my new theory: Mr. Morgan rips off the Longfellow, sells it in Boston, and then also collects the insurance money. . . . He waits until this weekend to grab it because it fits right in with his scheduled trip, and he knows the place is going to be full of potential culprits." E.T. put special emphasis on the newest addition to his vocabulary. "And listen to this: he tells *me* to go out back and shovel the kitchen steps, and then *he* sneaks out the front door; probably with the frame all wrapped up and everything. . . . Because when I was done with the steps he was long gone. And footsteps in the snow show that he definitely visited the trunk of his car before driving off."

Rosco gave the boy a pat on the back. "It's a theory, E.T., but I'm not certain it holds water. Mr. Morgan is just as worried about the theft as his brother."

E.T. frowned as if he wasn't certain this were the case.

"Besides," Rosco continued, "people don't generally steal from themselves . . . at least, not any I've found." Then he added a conciliatory "On the other hand, Mr. Morgan's absence will provide plenty of opportunity to question the guests. Mr. Mitchell's gathering them in the parlor for me."

Belle looked at her watch. "Mitchell figured that most of the overnighters would be ready for some re-freshments right about now."

"Good thinking," E.T. agreed, giving Belle a thumbs-up signal. "This is when Joy sets up the cocoa and cookies and stuff." He snapped his fingers. "She's another one we should be wary of. I've seen her dusting the poem, and spending a long time doing it, too. Very—and I mean *very*—suspicious. She may have only been trying to figure out how to get it off the wall." Then he jammed his hat back on his head and pulled down the ear-flaps. "Well, I've got more shoveling to do. . . . Call me if you need me."

"Roger," was Rosco's mock-serious reply as he and Belle shared an amused look and entered the inn.

The first thing that struck them as they stepped into the space was its lack of animation. The day before, all had been noise, excitement, and motion; now silence reigned supreme. The utter stillness made the old building seem strangely eerie and forbidding.

"I've asked the guests to assemble in the front parlor, Rosco." Mitchell's voice preceded him, as did the echo-ing sound of his footfall as he approached the couple. "I encouraged the decorating clubs to leave a short while ago. I hope that's acceptable. I felt that since we knew the participants fairly well, there was no sense in having someone risk a fender-bender or worse simply to answer questions. . . ." Then his habitual ambivalence and insecurity got the better of him. "The decorators will return tomorrow, however, after the snow plows have done their work. I'm sure f-f-folks will be happy to talk to you then. . . ."

"That's fine, Mitch." Rosco's assured tone seemed to relieve Mitchell Marz, and he also assumed a purposeful air, quickly explaining that only five of the inn's ten rooms were booked, and that because of the inclement weather, the three couples and two single guests had remained and were available for questioning. "They're as shocked about this situation as Morgan and I are," he concluded. "I can't imagine any of them had anything to do with the theft."

"What about employees?" Rosco asked.

"Except for Joy Allman, everyone has been with us for well over five years; and Joy's been here three."

"While we're waiting for your guests to assemble, Mitch, why don't you run through your list of employees. Would you suspect any of them at all?"

Mitchell shook his head. "First off, we have to look at opportunity. There was hardly anyone on duty when the poem disappeared—which was put at between midnight and nine—or rather 8:56—this morning when E.T. made his discovery. There's Chef; he's live-in; he has a one-bedroom above the current garage. And Joy was in early to set up breakfast."

"That's it?" Belle asked.

"For early morning staff, yes. Morgan has a separate

apartment with a separate entrance at the building's rear. I live in a small converted spring house on the premises. We can be easily summoned if there's a need, but no one else had arrived. We do a brisk lunch and dinner business, but the dishwashers and waitstaff don't start work until ten thirty or eleven. Our pastry cook generally begins around nine thirty."

"Do any of them have keys to the inn?" Rosco asked.

"No . . . just Chef and Joy. . . . And of course the hotel guests have a key to the front door."

"And, naturally, any former guest could have made a copy of the front door key," Rosco pondered aloud while Belle excused herself. By prior arrangement, she and Rosco had decided that she would do some quiet snooping while Rosco queried the guests.

As she walked away she almost ran smack-dab into a short but determined older woman who sported a gray helmet of hair that looked as hard and unforgiving as steel. "Hatchet-faced" would have best described her less-than-sunny countenance. "Are you trying to roll right over me, tootsie? Watch where you're going," she barked at Belle while Mitchell cooed a pleasant, "Ah, Miss Cadburrie, so nice of you to join us."

But before he could introduce this problematic person to Rosco, several other guests appeared. Within a moment, all eight were gathered in the parlor: the three couples, Miss Cadburrie, and a single gentleman by the name of Barry Heath. He was clearly the most ill at ease of the group. A tall, hulking man with close-cropped hair and a bushy mustache that was obviously an object of much veneration, his hands shook as if he had a permanent chill while his walrus-sized mustache danced with a nervous tic.

Where to start? Rosco wondered as he watched the assembled guests help themselves to cocoa, tea, or coffee. *How about a lie . . . ? It's as good a place as any to begin. . . .* "Let me first state," he said as seats were taken and cups and saucers placed nearby, "that none of you is a suspect in the theft. I'm simply asking for your suggestions and observations. You've had almost a full day to absorb the situation, and I was hoping one or more of you might have noticed something odd—either the behavior of the staff, or perhaps of the locals decorating the inn. I gather you've all stayed at the inn many times in the past?"

"Well, no," Mitchell interrupted. "Mr. and Mrs. Towbler are here for the first time, as is Mr. Heath. The Yorkes are with us for their second stay."

"I never arise before ten A.M.," Barry Heath interjected, "I didn't see anything, and the crisis was over by the time I came down for breakfast. My comings and goings have been witnessed by all."

The Towblers sat straighter in their chairs, sensing that being "first-timers" at the inn placed them outside the trusted loop. "I must say," Mr. Towbler began with a clipped, old-school British accent, "that my wife and I are as disappointed with this tragic scenario as anyone could be. As Mr. Marz can attest, we arrived here late last night, and like Mr. Heath, we awakened to find the poem had already gone missing. Neither one of us had an opportunity to even view it."

"And to be quite honest," his wife added, "that was one of the reasons we'd chosen the Revere Inn." She spoke with the same cultured accent as her husband. Like him, she also appeared to be in her mid fifties and was dressed in similarly conservative—and expensive— London tweeds.

"May I ask what you do for a living, Mr. Towbler?" Rosco said.

"Do?" was his irked reply.

"Yes . . . I was wondering what field you might be in."

Towbler cleared his throat, but it was his wife who answered. "We are fortunate enough to be independently wealthy, Mr. Polycrates. What we *do* is travel. We reside not far from Craigie House in Cambridge, England . . . where I'm sure you're aware Mr. Longfellow spent his final years. It has long been our desire to visit the spots that the poet most stirringly evoked. . . . We residents from 'across the pond' believe in lauding our noble *artistes*." She graced the gathering with a smile that expressed her sympathy for the poor, uncultured colonials who didn't support the arts.

"I see." Rosco turned his attention to another couple who were closer to his own age. They had the wholesomeness of avid sports enthusiasts, and they looked almost disturbingly similar: two round-faced blonds with pink cheeks and eyes as pale as snow. "How about you, Mr. and Mrs. Yorke? Has anything struck you as out of the ordinary? Either today or yesterday? Plainly, a theft such as this took planning."

The husband finished what was left of his cocoa and set the cup on the Queen Anne table beside him. Of the assembled group, he seemed the most relaxed and confident. "Our room is directly above this one." He pointed toward the ceiling. "And yes, I did hear an odd noise last night. I'd venture to say that was when the poem was stolen, but I never put two and two together. I'm embarrassed to say I didn't notice the time."

"Can you ballpark it?" Rosco asked. "Would it have been closer to midnight . . . or early in the morning?"

"I got up at four A.M. to take a look at the Milky Way. It was incredibly well-defined. . . . The noise from downstairs definitely came after that point, and I was awake at seven, so I feel safe in saying it was stolen between those hours. But as far as suspicious behavior . . ." He shrugged and looked at his wife. "How about you, Patty?" She shook her head, but made no other comment.

Rosco glanced at Miss Cadburrie, then asked, "And you, Mr. Heath?" without looking in that guest's direction.

"What? What about me? I didn't take it."

Rosco gave him a level gaze. "I didn't say you had. I was just wondering if you noticed any of the staff behaving oddly."

"Maybe you should be grilling them, and leaving the paying guests alone." Barry Heath's voice was hard but also unexpectedly brittle, as if his tense demeanor were about to break apart.

"I hope you don't feel I'm *grilling* anyone."

"It's an insult, that's what it is. I won't come to a place and be accused of behaving like a common criminal." Heath insisted.

"I agree with you, there, sport." This was Mr. Reasey speaking, and his twangy accent revealed him as a confirmed Down-Easter. He and his wife were seated on a couch at the far corner of the parlor, lumped together like two Maine potatoes. "My wife and I are going to have to excuse ourselves before this meeting becomes any more uncomfortable. We've stayed at the inn numerous times, and we have nothing to add with regard to observations of suspicious behavior. It seems to me you should be questioning the hordes of local people who've been swarming over the place. However, if we think of anything, Mr. Marz, we'll be certain to tell you." Rosco's name was conspicuously absent from this huffy speech, as if Reasey couldn't abide using a Greek surname. Then he stood, hefting his bulk from the low, antique sofa, and looked down at his equally chunky wife. "Coming, Ruth baby?" *Ruth baby* immediately struggled to her own square feet and waddled out the door after her husband.

The rest of the guests took this as their cue to leave as well. Within a matter of two minutes, Rosco found himself alone in the parlor with Mitchell and Miss Cadburrie. To say she was relishing her moment in the limelight would be an understatement; her eyes positively shone with malicious joy. "I, for one, don't find your line of questioning in the least bit intrusive, Mr. Polycrates. After all, how can one be expected to resolve this enigma if sensible people can't ask sensible questions?" She paused, her point made and handily won. "In my opinion, Mr. Polycrates, the Towbler duo are outright phonies, with their endless chattering about 'spots of tea' and 'Lord and Lady Snootypoo'. . . . I believe a search of their room will settle the predicament once and for all."

"Thank you, Miss Cadburrie." Rosco smiled benignly as he spoke. The Miss Cadburries of the world were best handled with caution lest they turn and snap at the people who'd befriended them. "I'll certainly keep your recommendation in mind, but without authority and a proper search warrant, I can't move forward as aggressively as I might want to."

A dismissive sniff greeted this statement. "You don't look like a person to be cowed by name-dropping and references to *Debrett's Peerage*. . . . I certainly hope you don't share the same *laissez-faire* approach to those appalling people from Maine. They're as common as dirt. Although, at least there's nothing sham about *their* pose."

Rosco merely nodded, while Mitch uttered a conciliatory, "Thank you so much for your aid, Miss Cadburrie. You know what a pleasure it is to have you stay with us."

The cantankerous lady softened, but the transformation only extended to Mitchell. "Well, I wanted to relay my thoughts in private, Mr. Marz, so as to not alert any—"

"Thank you for your help, ma'am," Rosco interrupted. He shook the lady's cool and papery hand to indicate that the conversation was concluded, then he watched her spin irritably on her heel and march away before he turned his attention to Mitchell. "I'd like to question the two employees who were on the premises when the poem disappeared, if that's convenient."

"You'll find Chef in the kitchen. But Joy didn't come in until seven this morning, so she's in the clear." Rosco said nothing, and Mitch added, "Because Yorke heard noises down here before seven, remember?"

"Right. Assuming he has no reason to lie."

Eleven

"I can recite the whole thing," E.T. boasted as he trailed behind Belle. With Mitchell ensconced with the guests in the front parlor, and Morgan temporarily out of the picture, E.T. had forsaken his outdoor duties in order to "help" Belle in her private hunt through the inn.

"What 'thing'?" she said, although she was hardly listening to her chatty escort. For the ten or fifteen minutes E.T. had been with her, she doubted he'd stopped talking for more than a second.

She depressed the antique iron latch of a door under the second-floor stairway and found it locked—the third such discovery she'd made, not including the closed guest bedrooms. *Someone,* Belle thought, *must pos-*

sess a good many old keys. "Are these closet doors usually locked?" she asked.

"I don't know, I never come up here. Mr. Morgan likes me to stay outside. I think he's afraid I'll break something. . . . So, do you want to hear me recite it?"

"Recite what?" Belle walked the length of the hall, then turned and walked down two steps that led to another section of corridor and another part of the building.

"The poem, of course!" E.T. exclaimed. Then he raised a hand and rapped himself on the head in a gesture of impatience. It was the sort of half-teasing, half-serious reminder an older kid would give a younger one. "You're right! Saying 'thing' and 'it.' That's totally dumb. Use *specifics*. The teachers at school are always telling us that . . . I guess you know *specific* is related to species. I looked it up in the dictionary. *Spy*'s another one, and so is *specter.* . . . You could say, 'I spy a specific species of speckled specters,' and be using words from the same family. Except for *speckled,* of course."

Belle chuckled, turning to face him. "Since when do ghosts sport spots?"

"It's hypothetical . . ." In the corridor's dim light, E.T.'s already serious face grew more so. "Actually, it's a mnemonic—"

"And you're now going to explain that those memory aids are named after the Greek titan, Mnemosyne, who was in charge of such cerebral doings—and who became the mother of the Muses."

"Yup." A bright grin lit up E.T.'s face.

"I'd better be careful or you're going to take my job away from me."

"I can't, 'cause I'm only twelve," was the sensible reply. Then E.T. repeated his previous offer. "So do you want me to recite the poem? I know the whole thing!"

The boy's need for approval and human connection was so evident that Belle felt instant empathy. "Your parents must be awfully proud of you," she told him.

But this accolade only brought a swift glower, followed by an evasive and defensive, "How come a bunch of lions is called a *pride* instead of a *herd* or a *flock?*"

"I don't know the answer to that one," Belle said as she scrutinized E.T.'s now uncommunicative face. "Maybe the king of the jungle would be insulted if someone insisted he was *sheepish* . . . or a *silly goose.*"

"If I were a lion and someone called me stupid names, I'd bite them," E.T. insisted, then his closed and somber expression vanished as noise of a boisterous arrival raced up the stairs. "It's the chocolate village!" he exclaimed with a sudden smile. "I didn't think Mr. Karl and his dad would get here to install it today on account of the snow. The staff—that's me—gets to eat the people and animals and everything at the end of the holidays. The registered guests are given a chocolate house or barn or something." Then E.T. roared away, a twelve-year-old boy focusing solely on childhood pleasures.

THE chocolate village scene was indeed a wonderful creation. Belle watched as the buildings and their inhabitants were assembled on a swirling blanket of white chocolate: the houses, constructed as fancifully as their gingerbread counterparts, interspersed on the wintry scene; the cookie trees thoughtfully arranged; the horses and buggies; the cows in their stalls; the sheep dotting the fields; and a dusting of confectioner's sugar sprinkled, like snow, over the entire panorama.

It was a sweet-lover's delight. "Didn't I tell you?" E.T. demanded. "Didn't I? Didn't I?" His eyes were focused on the magic scene. "And it really tastes great, too. Mr. Karl says it's because they use only the best ingredients. He told me I can watch them making it one day, and eat whatever I want. . . . Chocolate comes from cacao seeds, which grow in rain forests like the ones in Latin America. Ancient Mayas and Aztecs made a spicy drink out of it and mixed the seeds with incense offerings to the gods. . . . I looked up all that stuff in the encyclopedia at school. . . . Cortez, he was a Spanish explorer; he found storerooms full of cacao seeds instead of gold. That's how valuable the stuff was . . ."

Belle nodded as E.T. continued to reel off additional facts, and as the inn's guests gathered around the table upon which Legendary's scene was being displayed. Rosco and Mitchell were not among the group, and Belle heard a number of grumbles and downright critiques of her husband's handling of the investigation. She kept her mouth shut, and fortunately E.T. was so intent on his own running commentary that he didn't respond to the accusations either.

". . . The Aztecs and Mayas called it *chocolatl.* . . . You can use that in one of your puzzles, Belle. It's spelled—"

"*Chocolatl,*" old Mr. Liebig echoed as he crossed behind the group, the better to judge the sightlines of the delectable creation. Then he suddenly stopped and stared at Belle.

"Her husband was from the Netherlands," he stated quite plainly.

Belle didn't need to ask who the *her* was. She knew in a trice that the old man was referring to the mystery crossword cookbook constructor.

"And her name was . . . was . . . was . . . Swerve."

"Swerve?" Belle asked. It was no surname—or given name—she'd ever heard of. She tried to imagine what an appropriate synonym might be. "Do you mean Dodge, perhaps, Mr. Liebig?"

"Why would a person be named after a car?" was his perplexed reply. Then his face assumed a bright but mindless smile, indicating that the entire subject was now forgotten.

Twelve

THEY spoke while sitting in total darkness. The pitch-black seemed to contribute to their sense of seclusion and privacy; however, a certain paranoia arose from the fact that she couldn't see his face and eyes, or accurately interpret his expressions. Likewise, he couldn't read hers. No hand gestures, deceitful squints, or raised eyebrows were shared. As a result, distrust and tension infused each of their hushed words.

"And how do you propose we get the blessed thing out of the inn?" she snapped in a tired voice. "How? That's what I want to know. Our snow-shoveling, underage snoop has every vehicle in the lot under the watch of his beady little eyes. You heard the brat bragging to Polycrates. We couldn't go near a single one of those cars without there being a headline about it the *Boston Globe* tomorrow morning."

"Relax, will you? I'm not going to throw in the towel. There still has to be a way to pull this off. We're almost home."

"Ha! You had this so well planned, didn't you? *Mr. I've Thought Of Everything,*" was her facetious reply. "This is Massachusetts in November, you dope; you should have factored in the possibility of a snowstorm when you worked out your *brilliant* strategy—for as long as you've lived in New England? For as long as *I've* lived in New England?" She shook her head from side to side for effect, forgetting that he couldn't see it. "Neither one of us thought of snow . . . which leaves us trapped with the goods sitting in our laps."

"Okay, okay, I don't need to be lectured about this. So it snowed. So what? We move to plan B. We'll just have to carry the thing out when we leave. Sneak it through the kitchen or something; use the side door, maybe. One of us will stand guard, or create a distraction, that's all."

"You are so dense. You're worse than a block of firewood. I should have never agreed to go in on this with you. 'We'll just carry it out'? In what? A suitcase? The frame's almost twice as big as the ones we brought. It wouldn't even fit into one of those garland crates in the storage area; or that giant wreath box. . . . And everyone in the place is going to be watching the comings and goings like hawks until all the guests check out. Mitch has got this place in severe lockdown mode. . . . The only way to get it out is in the middle of the night. And with this snow, even that option's gone. We should have taken it straight out to the car last night like I said. But oh, no, you've got to 'give it the once-over' first. Now look where we are."

"Keep your voice down, will you? These doors are far from soundproof." He sucked in a big breath of air and let it out slowly. "Speaking of Mitch; do you think he knows the truth?"

"Maybe, maybe not. He was pretty young when this was all set up, right? It depends on what the old man said—and what Mitchell remembers."

The man drummed his fingernails on the desktop in front of him, not speaking for a long moment. Eventually he said, "I say we cut our losses and take a chance that no one remembers anything. At this point, it's the only way out."

"What're you talking about?" she demanded; but she did so cautiously, sensing she wouldn't like what was she was about to hear.

"I'm thinking we should settle for a smaller piece of the pie." He snickered to himself. "What do you say?"

"You mean bring someone else in on the deal? But there's already—"

"Relax. I didn't say anything about additional people, did I?"

"No, but—"

"It means a smaller payday, but we need to make some adjustments. There's still a lot of money to be made on the back end, remember? And I figure what Mitch doesn't know won't hurt him." He then explained his new plan to her, finishing by saying, "Get some sleep. We'll make our move at four A.M. And don't turn turtle on me; I can't do this without your help."

Thirteen

AT 8:29 the following morning, a yelp erupted from the inn's front parlor. The cry was followed by the crash and clatter of a cup and saucer falling to the floor, and the hurried footsteps of Morgan Marz running to the scene. In his hands were a stack of Sunday newspapers, which had arrived later than usual since there was now well over a foot of snow outside.

"It's back!" Mrs. Towbler burbled in her "Ox-Bridge" accent. "Or . . . well, I assume that's your famous poem hanging there."

Morgan only stared at the wall above the desk, while Mitchell entered the room followed immediately by Joy Allman, who was carrying a basket of freshly baked muffins.

"Why didn't you tell us?" Morgan asked her. "You know how concerned we've been."

"Tell you about what?" Joy serenely placed the hot muffins on a heating tray on the sideboard and then bent to pick up broken pieces of china. "Butterfingers, the lot of them," she grumbled, but softly enough so that Mrs. Towbler didn't hear.

"That the Longfellow was back!"

Joy straightened up slowly. She wasn't young, but neither was she old enough to have as stiff and sore a body as she now made a show of unbending. "Well, so it is," she announced when she'd achieved her full height. "What do you know about that!" Despite the enthusiastic words, she sounded more jaded than surprised.

"And decorated for the hols," Mrs. Towbler continued to babble brightly as she walked across the room to examine the framed poem, which was indeed now hung with tinsel and twinkling lights. "You clever, clever boys! This was a ruse to keep us snowbound folk entertained, wasn't it? Like one of those mystery weekends one reads about: a charming old inn, an unsolved crime, sinister shenanigans, creepy creaks on the staircase, and so forth. . . . I assume your Mr. Polycrates and that rather oafish policeman were actors hired to help move the plot along. They certainly did provide the necessary probing queries and clandestine, lowering of brows. . . . Is the little boy an actor, too . . . the one with the alien name? He should go far, that child . . . with all the kiddie movies Hollywood produces nowadays. He has a rather nice, if precocious, appeal."

At that moment, E.T. appeared, the earflaps on his hat flipped upward, lending him the appearance of a curious and determined puppy. He cast a quick, suspicious glance toward Joy Allman, and a more covert but equally leery one at Morgan, then walked purposefully toward the poem, staring at it long and hard.

"Oh, this is too marvelous!" Mrs. Towbler's tinkling voice gushed. "I must fetch my husband—and the others, of course. What fun! A genuine whodunit . . . but instead of Monsieur Poirot, we have Mr. Polycrates. Oh, my! I should have noticed the similarity yesterday—the P, the O, the R in the name of Christie's clever sleuth being reproduced in the Greek Polycrates. . . . Oh, you Americans, such an inventive race!" Then she turned to greet another arriving guest. "Ah, Miss Cadburrie. Do look at the fun gift we've been given! The inn's famous treasure has been miraculously reinstalled."

"What's all the hullabaloo?" the Yorkes asked in unison as they also walked into the parlor.

It was Miss Cadburrie who replied. Her tone was testy. "The Longfellow's back." She joined E.T., and began studying the poem with gimlet eyes—although not before she'd shot "the Brit" a superlatively nasty glance.

"But I d-d-don't understand," Mitchell Marz stuttered. "Who would have d-d-done this . . . ?"

"Done what?" It was the Reaseys turn to arrive on

the scene, and they also looked at the returned artwork with genuine surprise. "Well, my goodness, Ruthie baby . . ."

"The Marz twins have played a most entertaining hoax upon us," Mrs. Towbler told them.

"But I didn't—" Mitchell began as Miss Cadburrie quickly interrupted him.

"How do you know it was a hoax?" she demanded.

Mrs. Towbler gave the ill-tempered woman her sweetest and most condescending smile. "Whatever else could it have been, my dear lady, except a *divertisement* intended to enliven our visit? Something that's stolen doesn't magically reappear, does it? At least, at home that's not how cases of larceny work; a family heirloom is purloined, and that's the last one sees of it. Clearly, we were intended to solve "The Mystery of the Missing Manuscript" over dinner last night, and we all failed the test miserably." She laughed. "I must fetch my husband . . . and Mr. Heath, as well. Poor man, he was such a nervous wreck, yesterday—"

"Barry Heath told us he never gets up before ten," was Miss Cadburrie's chilly response, although Mrs. Towbler had already sailed from the room.

Fourteen

"So that's it? The missing poem was nothing but a *prank?*" Belle asked Rosco as she took careful aim, tossing a stick for Kit and Gabby to chase across the snowy grounds of the "dog park"—what had once been the spacious seaside lawns of the long-defunct Dew Drop Inn and that now served as a dog-run, toboggan-slalom, kite-flying arena, and all-around good-time gathering spot.

Rosco automatically ducked as the gnarled piece of wood took to the skies. If their years together had taught him only one thing about his wife, it was that she couldn't throw worth a darn. The stick was liable to go backward, straight up in the air, veer heavily to the right while she was facing left, or plop down a mere six feet in front of her. "Tricks" only a dog could love; anyone else would be best advised to wear protective head gear.

"Longfellow makes a surprise reappearance," Belle continued, "the guests disperse with smiles on their faces and a charming tale to tell to their neighbors. Ditto the decorators. Kind of a tempest in a teapot—or in this case, an antique Paul Revere tankard. If I hadn't seen for myself how concerned Mitchell Marz was, I'd wonder whether the entire scenario had been part of a publicity stunt. . . ." She gave Rosco a wry smile. "You don't have to duck, you know."

"I do if I don't want to be beaned in the noggin."

"Has one of my throws ever bopped you in the head?" she demanded in shocked surprise.

"You want me to answer that leading question for you, Poly-crates?" Al asked as he ambled through the snow to join the couple. With Al was Skippy, the butterscotch-colored labrador-shepherd-and-who-knew-what-else former stray who was the canine light of the homicide detective's life.

"Be my guest, Al."

Lever looked at Belle, and, as always, chickened out from voicing anything remotely resembling criticism. In his opinion, marrying the crossword editor was the best thing his former partner had ever done. "You see, Belle, we're all good at something. . . . Your skill happens to be with words, whereas your hubby and I . . .

well, let's just say we're more adept with the old sticks and stones."

Belle gave him a sardonic glance. " 'Sticks and stones may break my bones, but words can never hurt me'? Is that your inference?"

"I was thinking, 'The pen is mightier than the sword' kind of thing," was Al's quick retort.

"Flatterer," Belle laughed while Rosco shook his head.

"Talk softly and toss a big stick?" Rosco said. "Who knew this set-in-his-ways curmudgeon had it in him to go all sensitive and gooey?"

Al's response to this comment was a sheepish shrug. Then he picked up another ice-coated stick and threw it for Skippy to chase. "So, no more criminal investigation out at the inn, huh?" he asked, his eyes dotingly following the dog as he bounded away, kicking up foamy clouds of snow. Added to this backdrop of frolicking canines, friendly humans, sleds, plastic saucers, and a blur of kids' faces as they roared down the hill was a picture-perfect afternoon: the sky a cloudless cobalt blue, a lemon-colored sun, evergreens dense with white, and the wonderful stillness that follows any storm.

"Looks that way," Rosco answered, although he frowned as he spoke. "But there's still something weird about this. Morgan called me to tell me all was resolved—a 'prank,' bla, bla, bla . . . 'terribly sorry for wasting your time, but you know how easily Mitchell jumps to conclusions,' etc., etc. . . . Belle just mentioned that the whole thing could be a PR gimmick."

Lever nodded and again tossed the stick for the excited and now anxiously barking Skippy. "Could be . . . although publicity involving a supposed theft could backfire in a major way. . . . On the other hand—I'm sure it's entered your mind, Poly—Crates—the so-called crime might be no more than an escalating spat between the inn's two owners. Someone teaching someone else a lesson?"

Rosco paused a moment before speaking. "Yes, it has. The scenario goes something like this—and Belle can corroborate because she heard them having a similar argument just before the poem disappeared: Morgan's been increasingly concerned about protecting and insuring the inn's collection of antiques; he wants to dispense with the originals and replace them with reproductions. Mitch says ixnay—it's the real deal or nothing—which leads Morgan to pilfer the piece, albeit briefly, just to show his twin how easy it is for valuable antiques to 'walk.' Lesson learned: there's no point in keeping all those pricey collectibles around."

"I can't believe Morgan would play such a nasty trick on Mitchell," Belle said. "On the other hand, there was real tension between them the other day." As she spoke she pulled a well-worn tennis ball from Kit's mouth and drew her right arm back in preparation for a mighty throw. This time, both Rosco and Al flinched and ducked to the side. "Cowards," she chortled. "What's the point of tossing a ball if you know in advance where it's going to land?"

"There's a new concept for major league baseball," was Al's amused reply. "Instead of one guy at bat, you've got the whole team, and a pitcher firing off random curveballs."

"Which might help some of the pitiful underdogs get a run or two when they go up against the Sox," Rosco added.

Belle shook her head. "I hope you two realize how unbearably smug you've become since Boston *finally* won a World Series."

Their reaction to this accusation was to look even more self-satisfied, but Belle's expression grew suddenly serious, and her arm dropped to her side, much to Kit's disappointment. "The police department in Boston would keep homicide records dating from the 1940s, wouldn't it, Al?"

Lever looked at Belle. "What is it about your tone of voice that tells me I don't want to get involved in this?" was his cagey answer.

"But it would, wouldn't it?" she persisted.

Al turned to Rosco. "You've been hired to solve a *very* cold case up in Beantown? Is that it . . . ? Happy holidays. Find a murderer who whacked an innocent victim sixty-plus years ago. . . . My math makes that an octo-genarian executioner, Poly-crates—*if* the perps's still walking around."

"It's not Rosco, it's me," Belle said. "And it's not a murder, per se . . . although, it might be. . . ." She squinted in thought. "You see, I was visiting Legendary, and old Mr. Liebig told me about a woman who died af-ter falling into an enormous vat of chocolate—"

"This came up in ordinary conversation?" Al inter-rupted. "Doesn't sound like the kind of story most con-fectioners like to bandy about."

"Well, I was trying to discover the constructor of a mystery crossword cookbook I found at the Revere Inn."

"Hooo boy . . . ," Al half-cackled and half-groaned. "You didn't tell me your wife was on her puzzle-sleuth kick again, Poly-crates. This calls for a cigarette."

But as Al reached for the pack that was always close at hand, the arrival of Stanley Hatch's minivan made his fingers pause in midair while his jaw dropped. Belle and Rosco turned to see what Lever found so startling, and both had similar reactions. Because with Stan was not just his aging collie, Ace, but Martha Leonetti, who was now being carefully helped from the passenger seat by her solicitous driver. In Martha's arms was her Pekingese, Princess, who began licking Stanley's face as if he were her favorite human male on earth.

"Don't stare, you two," Belle whispered through

teeth clenched into a bright and hopefully noncommittal smile.

"She never brings Princess to the park in snow this deep," Al murmured back. "No matter what kind of outfit the dog's dolled up in."

"And I've never seen Stan looking so sappy—or so happy," Rosco added.

"Well, don't say a word," Belle continued to advise. "We'll act as though this were perfectly natural, and they always rode out here together. . . . Besides, remember what Stan confided to us yesterday, Rosco?"

Al gave Belle a questioning glance, but she pretended not to notice, and so the three friends merely watched Stanley and Martha walk toward them—with Ace parading regally beside the couple, and Princess, decked out in a quilted pink coat with white faux-fur trim, still held aloft in Martha's arms. Only the Peke looked uncomfortable with the arrangement, but her alarm seemed to focus on the expanse of chilly white. *You don't expect me to step in that icy stuff!* her bulging eyes seemed to demand.

"Great news about the poem," Stan said with a huge grin that didn't seem generated by Mr. Longfellow's works.

"Isn't it!" Martha's tone was so close to a simper that for a moment Belle and Rosco and Al couldn't speak. Salty-tongued Martha, cooing like a lovelorn teenager?

It simply wasn't possible. "All's well that ends well, I guess," she added in the same sweet and breathless voice.

"My motto exactly," Stan said, looking down on her with such a rapt expression that the other three felt they'd turned invisible.

"So true, Stanley," was Martha's soft response.

All this billing and cooing was beginning to make Al very restless; despite Belle's injunction to pretend nothing unusual was happening, he was about to make a pithy remark about two card-carrying AARP members people behaving like loopy kids when Rosco's cell phone rang.

The noise was a jarring note in the greeting-card scene, and Rosco's succinct "Polycrates" was equally abrupt and startling.

"It's E.T.," came the hasty reply. "I'm at the inn. You better come quick. I just figured it out. Somebody's tampered with the poem. Big time. I'll keep the info under my hat until you get here."

Fifteen

MOST adults would have listened politely to E.T.'s dramatic pronouncement that the Longfellow poem had been "altered" and written it off to a child's overly active imagination; clearly, if such had been the case, Mitchell and Morgan would have noticed the modification, too. But Rosco, who in his own youth had been accused on more than one occasion of inventing the same kind of wild theories, was inclined to pay attention. Besides, he found some plausibility in the boy's assertions—as well as a good deal of logic. What better explanation could there be than that the original poem had been replaced with a quality fake?

So after holstering his cell phone, Rosco trotted off to his Jeep, leaving Belle to enjoy the afternoon with her human and canine pals and a promise from Al to deliver her and "the girls" home safe and sound. As Rosco drove away he could see his former partner in the rearview mirror shaking his head and chuckling over Rosco's willingness to drop everything to pursue an off-the-wall "tip" from a "geeky kid."

Twenty-three minutes later Rosco was face-to-face with the same excited boy, a look of dark concentration in his eyes as he gazed at the framed poem. Standing to E.T.'s left was a bewildered Mitchell; to his right was a dour but equally confused Morgan. The holiday trappings with which Sisters in Stitches had festooned nearly every spare inch of the inn's front parlor seemed far too exuberant for the gravity of the occasion—and that included Sara's antique ornaments, which bobbed about beneath the pewter chandelier, set in motion by the creaking of the ancient ceiling beams and the equally aged floorboards. Rosco eyed the pointed silvery things, making a mental note not to try walking under the light fixture.

"See," E.T. insisted as he pointed to the seventh stanza. "See, right there, right after the line, *Meanwhile, impatient to mount and ride,* there's a semicolon."

"And your point is?" Morgan asked in a tight voice. He made no attempt to disguise the fact that he had better things to do than to spend time with a boy he'd hired to do the most menial of chores.

"So, that's wrong, Mr. Morgan," E.T. argued in a

manner that was both polite and self-righteous. "There should be a comma there, not a semicolon. That's so the reader doesn't take a big pause before going on to the next line, because it's the one describing what Paul Revere was doing—"

"I understand the difference between a semicolon and a comma, son," was Morgan's starchy reply.

Rosco interrupted before E.T. could make his own stubborn retort. "You're certain about the change?"

"Yes. I am." E.T.'s red hair bristled. "One hundred percent."

Rosco turned to Mitchell. "Do you have another copy of the poem? In a book, perhaps? Something we can check E.T.'s theory against?"

"Man, nobody ever believes me," E.T. grumbled. "I have the entire poem memorized—punctuation and everything . . .'cause it helps learn that stuff for school." He pointed again.

> *"Meanwhile, impatient to mount and ride,*
> *Booted and spurred, with a heavy stride*
> *On the opposite shore walked Paul Revere . . ."*

"See they're all commas. . . . So even if a book says the line's different, *this* copy has been tampered with. I know I'm right. I don't care what some other book says."

Rosco leaned in close to the frame and perused the

semicolon E.T. had indicated. He then ran his eyes around the frame, studying every inch carefully. After a moment he said, "If someone *has* replaced the original with a forgery, there'd be evidence of tampering on the back of the frame." He looked at Mitchell. "Do you mind if I take it down and see what the other side looks like?"

Mitch's "Fine by me" was quickly overlapped by Morgan's "Let's leave it where it is, Rosco. We all have work to do cleaning up after the decorators and tree-trimmers and what have you. The Longfellow's back in place. Let's just say we're glad it is and allow our little problem to disappear. Our *former* problem, I should say."

"Morgan," his brother responded with unaccustomed force, "I'd like to know what's going on. If someone has replaced the original with a fake, we have a right to know—and so does our insurance company." He patted E.T. on the shoulder. "There's a screwdriver and a pair of pliers in the center drawer of my desk. Would you get them for us?"

E.T. was off like a shot.

"This is a ridiculous waste of time, Mitch," Morgan argued.

"You're the one who decided to insure the poem for twelve thousand dollars," Mitchell fought back.

"We don't need to discuss whether or not the sum was an appropriate one in public. Besides, it was you who told me that the piece's true value couldn't be objectively calibrated. You said we had to bear in mind what it represented in terms of the inn's history—"

"All the same—"

Morgan's sigh of frustration curtailed his brother's speech. "All right, have it your own way. Let's wrench the thing off the wall, pry open the frame, and see if our anonymous jokester played fast and loose with Mr. Longfellow's punctuation marks . . . or whether our young, poem-loving snow-shoveler has made the tiniest of errors. . . . However, I suggest we try not to mar that nice antique desk in the process. I believe it's one of your favorite pieces, Mitchell."

"If I might interrupt," Rosco stated calmly. "I'm no expert on printed artwork, so I can't tell you whether someone replaced your original with a darned good fake, Morgan, but I do know that the framing has been tampered with. The poem wasn't simply taken and then returned intact."

Morgan grew quiet, although his irritation still glimmered below the surface. "What makes you believe that?"

"Here." Rosco pointed to the lower left-hand corner of the frame. "You can see that the marks on the glass left by years of cleaning don't quite match up with the edge of the framing any longer. There's been some slight movement."

Morgan nodded, his expression now inquiring but

still just as aggravated. "Well, perhaps whoever our prankster was jostled the frame—which caused the glass to move."

"I agree, that's a possibility," Rosco answered after a moment, "but if that were the case, we'd see evidence of movement at the *top* of the frame, not the bottom. Gravity would make the glass drop, not rise. It's my feeling that since the glass has risen slightly, the frame was laid flat and the backing removed, therefore relieving the tension between glass and frame."

E.T. came bounding in with the screwdriver and pliers clutched in his left hand. "Got it."

"You shouldn't run with a screwdriver in your hand, E.T.," Rosco advised. "It's very dangerous. What if you'd tripped?"

"But this was an emergency!"

"Not that much of one. The poem isn't going anywhere." Rosco took the screwdriver, handed it to Mitchell, and placed the pliers in his back pocket. "Why don't you loosen the wall screws, Mitch, while I hold the frame to keep it from falling."

As Mitchell worked on the screws, he said, "Well, this is certainly a two-man operation. That lets our single guests off the hook."

"As it were," Rosco couldn't help but add.

"Unless . . . Mr. Heath and Miss Cadburrie were working together," E.T. observed as he rubbed his chin and furrowed his brow. This, combined with the snow hat still stuck on his head, made him look like a miniature version of Sherlock Holmes. He began to pace the antique Oriental rug. "Both of them were acting weird when they checked out, didn't you think, Mr. Mitchell?"

"To tell you the truth, E.T., I didn't notice," was Mitch's distracted reply while Morgan added an impatient:

"Well, I did. Their checkout times had a two-hour differential. And I don't believe I saw them say more than a few words to each other for the entire weekend."

But E.T. wasn't about to give up. "My point exactly, Mr. Morgan. . . . All very suspicious behavior, very suspicious."

The twelve-year-old's solemn tone made Rosco smile to himself as he took the frame from the wall and laid it facedown on the carpet. As he straightened he said, "There's your answer. The paper backing is completely gone. Cut clean, very smoothly; probably with a razor or sharp knife."

The other three stared down at the back of the frame.

"I told you so!" E.T. said proudly. "Someone put a phony in there. I'll bet you a hundred dollars."

"My hunch is that's not going to be the case, E.T.," Rosco said as he bent over once again and began to pull the retaining nails from the sides of the frame with the pair of pliers. "I think what we're seeing on the poem is simply a speck of dirt just above the comma—which only makes it look like a semicolon. How, and why, the speck got there is now the big question."

After he'd removed the last nail, Rosco lifted the backing board from the frame. This exposed another thin, flat inner frame, about an eighth of an inch thick and an inch wide all around. It was fashioned from wood and had a wood backing. Rosco also removed this inner pocket, then carefully lifted the poem and turned it over. The semicolon E.T. had pointed out still existed, but the moment Rosco blew lightly on the paper, the speck flew away, and the punctuation mark returned to its original comma.

"So it *is* the poem that's always been here . . . ," Mitchell said as bewilderment spread across his face. "Nothing's been stolen, after all. . . . But . . . but who would go through all these shenanigans simply to play a trick?"

Rosco picked up the inner frame. "I'm guessing that this served as a secret hiding place—meaning that there was something concealed behind the poem; something more valuable. Perhaps another piece of artwork or stock certificates or even cash."

"Or a treasure map!" E.T. chimed in.

Rosco gave him a conspiratorial nod. "Anything's possible."

Morgan turned toward Mitchell, then offered a reasonable "Well, whatever was behind the poem has been there since our father attached it to the wall back in the 1940s."

"You're certain of that?" Rosco asked.

"Absolutely," Mitchell answered for his twin. "Look at the screws that held it in place. Our dad shellacked them; that coating is now cracked, peeling and unsightly——"

"What my brother means is that he never would have condoned such a unfortunate mess," Morgan said, although the tone had become charitable rather than sarcastic.

Mitchell gave a small smile in response. "Visuals aside, Rosco, when our father placed the Longfellow here, he coated the screws with shellac. We were just kids then, so I couldn't tell you why he decided to attach the frame to the wall in such a semipermanent fashion. . . ." Then Mitchell looked at his twin brother. "I know what you're going to say. Anyone can throw on a coat of varnish; that the poem could have been removed on any number of previous occasions—when we were away in college, for instance. . . . But my point is that Dad must have had a reason for covering the screws with a material that would reveal if the piece had been disturbed . . . as a kind of . . . a kind of primitive warning device——"

"More hidden treasure maps, huh?" Morgan chided. The tone had grown less kind.

"Dad didn't know he was going to die when he did,

Morgan! Maybe he did possess something of value, and felt that this spot was—"

"What he had was this property, Mitchell, a couple of youngsters, and a wife who worked her fingers to the bone to keep up the—"

"Well, someone knew about this secret compartment." Rosco interrupted the brothers before their argument could intensify.

Morgan released an irate snort. "It wasn't us!"

"I'm not accusing you or Mitch of anything," Rosco answered. "I just think it would help if we all knew what sort of thing were looking for."

It was Mitchell who next spoke. "I'm afraid we can't help you, Rosco. If our father did hide something behind the Longfellow, the knowledge died with him. Of course, it's possible that he confided in our mother, but . . . but I can assure you that she never shared the fact with us. . . ." In his effort to be helpful, Mitch again began to trip over his words. "After all, whatever D-D-Dad concealed there would belong to both Morgan and me now. And we w-w-wouldn't . . . well, we wouldn't have any cause to steal from ourselves, would we? And . . . and after nearly sixty years . . . ? We would have removed it long ago if we'd known."

Rosco nodded. "You may not know what was stashed here, but someone possessed information about this secret compartment. Either that person found old correspondence detailing it, or they talked to a third party who knew about it. However the theft came about, it's clear that our culprit was able to obtain specific facts that led directly to this poem. And I'm assuming the discovery was made fairly recently. Otherwise, you're absolutely correct, Mitch, this would have occurred long ago."

"But why not steal the Longfellow, too?" Mitchell asked. "Why go through all this pretense and then return it as if the deed were no more than a prank?"

"Maybe the snowfall forced the thief—or thieves—to alter their plans," Rosco told him. "Or perhaps, leaving the poem behind was the intention, all along. After all, neither of you questioned whether the back of the frame had been disturbed. If E.T. hadn't spotted that rogue semicolon, the mystery might have gone unnoticed for another sixty years."

Rosco lifted the inner compartment from the carpet and carefully rested it on the desktop. Then he pulled a chair close and seated himself while E.T. perched beside him and also began staring silently at the frame.

"I don't appreciate the insinuation that Mitchell or I were—or *are*—involved in this bizarre situation," Morgan said after a long moment.

"I didn't suggest anything of the kind," was Rosco's quiet answer. Then he stood and began walking toward the door. "But someone is."

Sixteen

THE moment Rosco and the two "girls" returned from their early Monday morning run, the phone rang. Belle, accoutered in corduroy trousers, a cotton turtleneck, and her beloved Irish fisherman's sweater—all of which were dry and cozy—answered it while Rosco toweled off the drenched and bedraggled dogs. He then shucked off his own soggy running shoes and peeled the road-salt–spattered waterproof pants from his sweats. The discarded clothing fell in a heap by the door, as the dogs gave one final dramatic shake to punctuate their entrance.

"No, no, it's not too early at all, Stan," Rosco heard Belle say before she cupped the receiver and mouthed an unnecessary *It's Stanley Hatch. For you.* Then she held out the phone, straight-arm fashion, as if her husband's sodden state were contagious and her nice, fluffy slippers might turn into grimy puddles if she stood too close. *Coffee now or after your shower?* she also mouthed, but Rosco was too intent on the information Stanley was delivering to reply.

"Can you spell that name for me, Stan? Is it a U or an E-W?" Rosco cradled the phone as he reached for a pad of paper. "Uh . . . huh . . . And he was a buddy of the twins' dad . . . ? Okay, yep . . . I got it. . . . And that's near Boston, I guess? On the way to Hull? Oh, yeah . . . ? Well, tell her 'hi' from me. . . .""

By now curiosity had turned Belle's eyes into gray-black slits, and any notion of contagious sleet-water had evaporated. *Who?* she mouthed. *Where is Stan? What's going on?*

But Rosco's sole response was to reply with his own silent *Lawson's,* and to mimic eating breakfast. Belle almost swatted him, but he continued to talk into the phone with maddeningly incomplete sentences before finally concluding with an equally enigmatic "Thanks, Stan. . . . Hopefully he can fill in some missing pieces."

The receiver was only halfway to its cradle when Belle demanded a rapid "What? What pieces? And who's the mystery *her* you're saying hi to?"

"Martha," Rosco answered, as though nothing could be more obvious. "Stanley was calling from Lawson's, where he's having breakfast. She told him that the poem's frame had a secret compartment, and that what-ever was in it is missing."

"How did she—?" Belle began then stopped herself. Martha Leonetti knew virtually everything that happened in Newcastle; and the speed with which she gathered her facts was often truly startling. But then, Lawson's was Newcastle's favorite hangout for cops, DAs, judges, lawyers as well as the common citizenry, and Martha was not famed for her reticence or for the subtlety of her questions.

"So Stan called to tell me about a war-time buddy of Mike Marz—"

"The M and M's dad. . . ."

Rosco nodded. "The guy's name is Charlie Chew, and he's in a retirement community on the outskirts of Boston. He and Mike were thick as thieves after they came home from Europe, and Stan figures if anyone knows what Mike might have hidden behind the poem, it could be Mr. Chew."

Belle had a image of old Karl Liebig and his on-again-off-again memory, but Rosco beat her to the punch. "Stan says Charlie's not only as sharp as a tack, but one of the nicest folks you'd ever want to meet. Stan's been up there to visit on several occasions, but not since his own father passed away."

"Well, we'd better get a move on." Belle was already at the coat closet and pulling out her boots.

"What's this 'we' business?"

"Subcontractor of the Polycrates Agency, that's me, remember?"

Rosco's response was a mock sigh. "How could I forget?"

"Besides, you know how fabulously I get along with people of a certain generation."

Rosco shook his head. "Mind if I put some real trousers and shoes on before we get rolling?"

"That was my next suggestion," Belle said with a gleeful grin. "Oh, and maybe we should have breakfast, too. No point in forgetting a meal as important as that, is there?"

BY conventional standards, the Nantasket Retirement Community, or NRC as it was known to its residents, was a giant step above the average old-age home. It overlooked Hingham Bay, which was seven miles southeast of Boston's Logan Airport, making it convenient for out-of-town visiting relatives; although jet noise was an occasional irritant for the residents. As this depended largely on wind direction and landing patterns, the place could also be quietness itself: a vista revealing an expanse of sea water, a few gulls lofting along with the breezes, and a collection of ships and sailboats attractively decorating the distance.

Nantasket's main building consisted of a one-story structure fashioned from honey-colored bricks with sixty private suite apartments stretching along the cliff's edge in a wide V pattern; thirty on either side of the central reception area. An enclosed walkway led to a spacious dining room that also had a partial seaside view, a workout room, a recreational lounge and library, a unisex hair salon, and an exercise pool. It was designed for active older people, the "fifty-five plus" crowd who enjoyed whipping up special meals in their private kitchens. Many still owned and drove their own cars. And although there was a nursing staff on duty at all times, the residents were more than capable of functioning independently.

For those whose health and cognitive skills had declined, and who required more sophisticated medical facilities and an expanded professional staff, NRC-2 lay across the street. Charlie Chew was emphatically not a resident of NRC-2. At eighty-four years of age, he was as hale and hearty as he'd been when he'd been a "mere stripling" of sixty.

Belle and Rosco entered the retirement community's reception area just before noon. It had already been tastefully decorated for the holidays with garlands woven out of pine and cedar. A manger scene had been set up on the left side of the entry and a menorah to the right, and a large balsam pine tree had been placed in the center of the lounge.

No ornaments had yet been hung on the tree, but a

number of cardboard boxes sat at its base along with an aluminum stepladder.

"This is a nice setup," Rosco said to Belle as they walked toward a young red-haired woman sitting behind a long granite-topped reception desk. "It looks like our Mr. Chew has done well for himself."

A nameplate on the counter read "Kitty Katlyn, RN," but the woman was not outfitted in a nurse's uniform; instead she wore a demure blue suit and striped blouse.

"We're here to see Mr. Chew," Rosco said. "He's expecting us; Rosco Polycrates and Belle Graham."

"I'd recognize that face anywhere," Charlie Chew nearly shouted from across the room. He was as tall as Rosco, thin and angular, and walked erect and with the confidence of a person who had spent a lifetime being in charge of most situations. "I'm a true crossword junkie, Ms. Graham," he continued. "I have every one of your annual collections. First thing I do is rip the answer pages out of the back and feed them to the paper shredder."

"Bravo," Belle said with a pleased smile. "But please call me Belle. This is my husband, Rosco."

"I would have guessed that. News of your investigations does reach us in the NRC, but you've sure done a good job of keeping your mug out of the papers, Rosco. I somehow envisioned you as more of a bookish type, but you look like someone who can handle himself physically. Brawn *and* brain." They shook hands. "Why don't we step into the lounge. Most folks are having lunch right about now. We shouldn't be disturbed there."

"We hate to make you miss your meal," Belle said.

"Heck, I don't eat lunch. . . . Never have. A healthy breakfast and a solid dinner; that's it for me. Lunch? Espresso and a cigar, and I save that for three in the afternoon when most folks are taking a nap."

Once in the lounge, Belle and Rosco sat together on a small tweedy couch while Charlie Chew chose a wing chair upholstered in the same nubby and clublike fabric.

"So," he said, "what's all this about?"

Rosco started. "A good friend of ours, Stanley Hatch—"

"*Stanley* Hatch is still around?" Charlie said with a laugh and a knee slap. "That old dog must be a hundred if he's a day. His son visits me once in a while. Young Stan, he's called. Hasn't been here in ages, though. Nice kid."

"Ah . . . actually, it's the son I'm referring to," Rosco said. He was about to add that *young* and *kid* might not be the optimal words to describe the current owner of Hatch's Hardware, but Charlie had intuited that on his own.

"Of course you are. I don't know what I was thinking there for a moment . . . Funny how names stick with you. *Young,* for a middle-aged guy. . . . Okay, so *this* Stanley Hatch, who's no longer as bright-eyed and bushy-tailed as he once was, is a buddy of yours, and . . . ?"

"He told us that back in the late forties you were a member of VFW Post 85 in Newcastle," Rosco continued. "And that a man by the name of Mike Marz had also joined?"

"We were more than fellow members," Charlie answered, his face losing some of its sparkle and his eyes misting slightly. "Mike and I fought side by side in Patton's Third Army throughout the war. The whole shebang: North Africa, France, and right into Germany. We were buddies all the way through. Thick and thin. Right up to that damn hunting accident after we came home. That was a bad time all around, I can tell you. The community did what they could to help. I remember a neighbor lady in particular who befriended Mike's widow . . . but it was tough; a young gal like that with two kids. I'm sure you know Mitch and Morgan. They own the inn now."

"Yes, we do," Belle offered after a moment. "Actually, that's why we're here. We're looking for someone who was close Mike, especially during the time *following* the war."

Charlie suddenly slumped in his chair. For a moment, it looked as though all the stuffing had been knocked out of him. "It's about that darn painting, isn't it?" he said in a muffled tone. "Rosco's a PI. He's been hired to find it. I should have figured that one out pronto." He sighed deeply and seemed to settle even lower into his seat. After another long moment, he spoke again. "I did consider ignoring that letter I received in October, considered playing dumb or pretending I'd never gotten it . . . but at my age . . . well, I wanted to purge the incident from my life. I wanted to see everything returned to the rightful owner. . . ."

Rosco and Belle hadn't a clue what Charlie Chew meant, but they chose to remain silent as though his words were only corroborating information they'd already been supplied.

"Am I right? The museum in Salzburg has put you on retainer to retrieve Mike's painting?" Charlie asked Rosco; and without waiting for a reply followed it with, "Sure, that makes sense; the museum figures I'm ducking them, so they put a pro on the case."

Belle glanced at her husband, but he made no response other than to gaze steadily into Charlie Chew's face.

"I may be an old man, but I know which end is up. Why else would you set up an appointment to interview me? Have you seen it? The portrait, I mean?"

"No. No, not yet," Rosco said, which wasn't technically a lie.

"Silly question. Of course, you haven't. From what

the curator wrote me, I gather no one has set eyes on it for a long, long time."

"Actually," Rosco said, clearing his throat and forging ahead with a spur-of-the-moment fib, "the curator in Salzburg didn't supply a heck of a lot of information. There was a language problem, and that heavy Austrian accent . . . Well, I'm still not sure I have all the details that clearly in our mind. This is why we opted to come to you directly."

"Well, I promise you I did respond to the initial letter the museum sent back in October. And their follow-up letter only arrived here on Friday. That's the first I realized things had gotten fouled up. Why my reply was never received on their end, I don't know. Must've been lost in the mail, but I explained everything I knew. I really wanted to come clean about this entire affair. It's gone on far too long."

"Since your correspondence to the curator was lost," Belle joined in, keeping up the deception, "he asked us to locate you and get the entire story firsthand."

"She," Charlie corrected. "The curator's a woman."

"She, of course," Belle covered with a quick smile. "I was thinking of her assistant, Herr Holtzelfritz. That's who Rosco has been dealing with."

Rosco refrained from rolling his eyes and said, "Maybe you could outline your involvement in this, Mr. Chew?"

"I . . . I just want to get it settled. That was my intention in October. I want everything to come out right."

"Everyone does, Mr. Chew," was Belle's quiet response.

"It all goes back to the war . . . toward the end. Like I said, Mike Marz and I were in the same platoon, and as we moved into southwest Germany we came across a fortified bunker. It was loaded with artwork: paintings, marble and bronze sculptures, even some tapestries. We had no idea the pieces had been moved there from Austria. Stolen, actually . . . Anyway, there were these two smallish paintings, a matching set. We didn't know how valuable they were. They were just nice pictures, pleasant souvenirs . . . One scene depicted a woman seated at the end of a rectangular table in an ornate parlor; in front of her was a fancy porcelain, hot-chocolate set. The other painting portrayed what looked to be her children; they were at the opposite end of the same table, anxiously waiting to be served their treat. Everyone was decked out in their finest."

"And you and Mike Marz decided to bring the two paintings home with you," Rosco said, more as a statement than a question.

"Yes. I'm certainly not proud of what we did, but we were younger, and . . . and we'd been through a lot, and somehow we just . . . well, we just grabbed them. We imagined the gesture keeping us bonded for life, like blood brothers. I kept the portrait of the mother—

although I didn't display it. Mike had the one of the kids. . . . It wasn't until I needed to make a down payment on my first home, and discovered I could sell my painting for three thousand dollars—which was a princely sum back then—that we learned what we had.

"Two genuine Henri-Paul Vénérers; mine was signed and dated 1760—making Vénérer a contemporary of Boucher, is what I was told. . . . The woman was Empress Maria Theresa of Austria; one of her children was none other than the five-year-old Marie Antoinette. And we all know what happened to her. . . . Needless to say, Mike was thrilled with my windfall. He planned to bring his portrait out of hiding and sell it, too, but then he was killed in that awful accident. . . ." Charlie released another heavy sigh, again pausing in troubled thought.

"I'm glad my Vénérer finally ended up back in the museum it was originally looted from. Really, I am. And Mike's should be there, too. . . . I know what we did was wrong, taking the pictures from that bunker . . . but after I'd sold mine, my career began to take off, and I didn't want to risk a scandal for myself or my family. . . ." Charlie shook his head. "What I should have done was tell Mike's widow right away; selling the portrait would have helped her financially. . . . But she was an awfully proud lady. It would have really hurt her to know that her husband had taken something that didn't belong to him, so I just . . . I just kept my trap shut, and left everything swept under the proverbial carpet."

"Until the museum recently acquired the painting of Maria Theresa, and decided to attempt to reunite her with her children?" Belle mused.

"Yes. They traced the one painting back to me. I swear I responded to their letter back in October," was the pensive reply. "I can't understand why they never received it."

"We have good reason to believe that Mike hid the painting behind the framed Longfellow poem that hung in the inn," Rosco said.

"Oh, I outlined all that in my letter," Charlie told him. "Everyone at the VFW post thought it was a huge joke that Mike clamped that old poem to the wall—like it was made of solid gold—but I knew better. I knew what was going on."

"So, all these years you were aware where the Vénérer was hidden?" Belle asked.

The old man squinted and stared into space. "Well, Mike never told me for certain that that was the spot he'd chosen, although it didn't take a brain trust to put two and two together. . . . I explained my suspicions in my response to the curator in October. I suggested she contact the Marz twins personally, but I asked her not to mention my name to the boys." Charlie ran his fingers through his white hair and shook his head. "I'm glad this has been finally settled. It's weighed on my conscience for sixty years. . . . I'd guess that painting's worth an awful lot of money now—especially with the two together. . . . I'd like to go with you when you pull the poem off the wall. I'd like to see the picture one last time before it's sent back to Austria . . . as a sort of memorial to Mike and what we went through together."

"There's a problem with that, Mr. Chew," Rosco said. "Someone's already beaten us to the punch. The portrait was stolen this week."

Charlie sat in absolute silence as he absorbed the information.

"Did you confide its location to anyone other than the curator?" Rosco continued. "Anyone in your family? Or an acquaintance here?"

The old man made several small clicking sounds with his mouth, and then finally said, "No. No one. I wrote the curator, but that was it."

"A letter which he . . . er, she, never received," Belle added.

"Did you take your letter directly to the post office? Was it registered?" Rosco asked.

"No. We leave all our correspondence at the front desk, and someone hands it off to—" Charlie paused once again. "Wait, you know what? I gave that letter to Reggie. He's a nurse here. His wife, MaryJane, too. They're terrific people, and genuine health nuts which is good for some of us. geezers . . . I remember asking Reggie to take it to the P.O. for me, because it was international mail and might require more postage than I'd affixed. I would have driven it over myself, but my grandson had borrowed my car for the Halloween weekend."

"I guess we should be talking to Reggie and Mary-Jane," Rosco said, almost to himself.

Charlie laughed. "What? You think they hijacked my letter?" He laughed again. "Reggie and MaryJane have been at the NRC for years. Besides teaching yoga and all that 'good diet' business, they handle our weekly entertainment. I hardly think they would do anything as outrageous as tampering with the mail, let alone stealing a painting."

"You never know."

"You're barking up the wrong tree, there, Rosco," Charlie continued, still chuckling. "Reg and MaryJane have this routine they do—Lord and Lady Battle-Axe, a couple of stuffy upper-class Brits who own a dilapidated castle near Cambridge. They have those accents down pat. It's ten times funnier than any of those Brit-coms you see on TV."

Rosco smiled thinly. "I'll bet it is. Actually, I have a strange feeling that I may have already caught part of their act. . . ."

But Charlie wasn't listening; instead he was pointing toward the hallway. "There's Reggie now. Let me get him over here and have him do some of his comedy bit for you. He'll have you in stitches." Charlie Chew stood and called across the room. "Reggie! Hey, Reg, come on over here. I've got some people I'd like you to meet. And grab MaryJane while you're at it."

Rosco walked to the door. "Mr. Towbler, I presume?"

Christmas, Current

Melt together over low heat: ¾ cup *21-Across;* 3 oz. *56-Across* + *22-Down;* ¼ *26-Across* butter . . . then cool to lukewarm

Lightly beat: 1 *38-Across;* ⅓ cup *16-Across;* and 1 tsp. vanilla

Stir the *38-Across* mixture into the *22-Down* mixture until blended

Sift together: 1 cup cake flour; 1 cup *49-Down;* ½ tsp. baking soda; a pinch of salt

Rapidly beat the flour mixture into the *22-Down* mixture until smooth

Stir in ½ cup *34-Across;* ¾ cup chopped pecans

Pour batter into greased and floured 9-by-4-inch loaf pan

Bake at 275 degrees for 45–55 minutes until firm but not completely dry

Cool in pan on a cake rack for 20 minutes before removing

This will serve 8–12

ACROSS

1. Chessman
6. Flap
7. Corn center
12. King of the fairies
14. Everything
15. Paddle
16. MAMA's DESSERT
18. Zodiac sign
19. Map; abbr.
20. Petites; abbr.
21. MAMA's DESSERT
24. Gift locale; apropos the tree
26. MAMA's DESSERT
27. North or South follower
28. Earthy color
31. Quarrels
34. MAMA's DESSERT
38. MAMA's DESSERT
39. 35-Down bubbles
41. Surprised exclamation
42. Grist
45. Boy's Christmas wish
47. Miss Shearer of the Silents
48. Steam
49. Gulf of _____ in the Aegean
52. Holiday news
56. MAMA's DESSERT
59. Lyric poem
61. Head of state; abbr.
62. Lyric poem
63. Badgering
65. Swiss peak
66. _____ & outs
67. Shed
68. Thing, in law

69. 23-Down lang.
70. Indian guitar

DOWN

1. Sailors
2. Biggest blast
3. North sea feeder
4. Goof
5. Highwaymen
6. Chatter
7. Herbert portrayer in "Great Expectations"
8. Radio goof
9. Ionian Island
10. Like some breads
11. Classification
13. Lloyd, of "Captain Eddie"
17. Slave leader Turner
22. MAMA's DESSERT
23. Roman marketplaces
25. Fisherman's aid
29. Slice
30. Kingly letters
31. Religious sch.
32. Ben Hogan's grp.
33. Ten percenter; abbr.
35. Holiday quaff
36. Calendar abbr.
37. Daughter's brother
39. Christmas tree, often
40. Butt
43. Poetic plenty
44. Attar
45. Spans
46. Big _____
48. Perfect
49. MAMA's DESSERT

🎄 *Christmas, Current* 🎄

1	2	3	4	5				6	7	8		9	10	11
12					13			14				15		
16						17		18				19		
20				21			22				23			
	24		25							26				
			27				28	29	30					
31	32	33				34					35	36	37
38				39	40						41		
42			43	44				45	46				
		47					48						
49	50	51				52	53				54	55	
56				57	58					59		60	
61			62				63		64				
65			66					67					
68			69					70					

50. Iguana relative
51. Polite replies; abbr.
53. Tavern
54. Flash of light
55. Mr. Claus
57. Miss Millay
58. Question

60. Frankenstein's assistant
64. Lively, in France

Seventeen

"Wow . . . so, Mr. Charleston Chew knew all about the pilfered painting? I could never keep a secret for sixty years. I mean, that's a really, really, really long time. . . . And it makes him an accessory to a crime, I guess, too, doesn't it?" E.T. was supposedly helping Belle prepare one of the crossword desserts as he spoke. In fact, what he was doing was scrutinizing the cookbook puzzles while munching away on some of the raw ingredients listed in "Christmas Current."

"It's Mr. *Charles* Chew, not Charleston, E.T." Belle chortled. "And if you don't stop sneaking pecans and currants, I'm not going to have enough to make this cake for Ms. Leonetti's holiday party."

"And I can go with you and Rosco? Like, really and truly? I've never been to a grown-up party before."

"If it's okay at home, it's fine with us." When E.T. failed to respond, Belle pressed him. "You did ask your folks, didn't you? The party's tomorrow night."

"Sure . . . yeah . . . I got approval and everything. . . ."

"Hmmm . . . You don't sound very sure, E.T."

"Well, I am!"

Belle studied the boy's face, uncertain whether or not to believe him, but he stared back with such an enigmatic expression that she gave up the effort. "You know, Rosco and I don't want to do anything that would upset your family," she said after a long moment.

His sole response was to shrug, as if suggesting that nothing would rattle the residents of his home, so Belle continued with a gentle, "Anyway, it's not going to be a really *grown-up* event. All the dogs are included, so I imagine Martha's place is going to be pretty chaotic. It gets crazy enough around here with just these two, so once you add Ace and Princess and the others, who knows what will happen?" As Belle made this observation, she looked affectionately at Kit and Gabby, who were curled around E.T.'s chair, snoozing peaceably. Twelve-year-old boys, she decided, must have a magnetic attraction for canines—and vice-versa.

E.T. reached down to stroke the two sleeping heads; his face was now full of doting concern. "Maybe we shouldn't be making this chocolate cake, then, Belle. Chocolate's poisonous to dogs. It's got something called theobromine in it. I looked it up—"

"I know, in the encyclopedia." Belle interrupted with a smile. "I promise we won't let any of them near the stuff." Then she cocked her head and regarded him with a mock serious expression. "However, I'm not certain *we* is the operative word for today's activity, because as far as I can figure, I'm doing all the work."

"I'm reading you the clues and answers, aren't I?"

"Hmmmm . . ." was Belle's noncommittal reply as she returned to concentrating on greasing and then flouring a loaf pan and checking to make certain the oven was set to preheat at 275 degrees. An avowed non-cook, her actions were slow and careful, like someone who's just learned to drive.

"So, is Lieutenant Lever going to arrest Charleston . . . um, Mr. Chew and the M and M's?" E.T. persisted with the kind of lugubrious delight also reserved for preteen boys.

"Not unless there's a murder involved," Belle answered as she broke an egg into another hand-me-down bowl and tried to decide what precisely was meant by "lightly" beating the yolk and white. "Lieutenant Lever's head of homicide, remember? Stolen goods aren't his domain. Besides, I imagine the statute of limitations may be expired."

"What kind of statue is that?" E.T. asked her.

"Pardon me?"

"What you were talking about . . . a statue of limitations. . . . Like, is it in a museum?"

Belle chuckled. "Aha, caught you, Mr. Dictionary! *Statute* is from Late Latin: *statutum,* for law."

E.T. scribbled the word in a composition notebook he had nearby, then stared at the letters, memorizing them. "So, if Lieutenant Lever discovered that the lady who drowned in the chocolate works was murdered instead of falling in by mistake, he couldn't do anything about it because of this statute?"

"Homicide's different," Belle explained. "But you know what? You can ask Lieutenant Lever all about that investigation yourself tomorrow. He was up in Boston yesterday going over old records. He'll be at Ms. Leonetti's, too. With his wife and his dog, Skippy."

"Cool!" was E.T.'s enthusiastic response. Belle imagined his excitement was meant for the four-legged member of the Lever family rather than for what Al had discovered in Boston; which was quite a bit more than old Mr. Liebig had remembered. The dead woman had, in fact, been murdered; pushed into the chocolate vat by a jealous lover who then tried to ship out with the merchant marine before the body was discovered. Unfortunately for him, his ship's departure was delayed by a week because a U-boat had been sighted lurking behind the Stellwagen Bank off Cape Cod, meaning that the perpetrator was dragged off the boat by the cops, tried, and convicted of murder in the first degree. On top of that, the deceased had been a Polish immigrant with only a marginal understanding of English, so any imagined connection Belle had created between the mystery woman and the cookbook was now null and void.

Belle released a brief, frustrated sigh, then returned her focus to the cake. "Okay, what's next?"

E.T. studied the crossword. "Um . . . let's see. . . . You're melting the 21-Across, 26-Across, 56-Across, and 22-Down over a low heat . . . ?"

"Three-quarters of a cup of *BLACK COFFEE* . . . one-quarter of a *POUND* of butter . . . three ounces of *UNSWEETENED CHOCOLATE*. . . . Yup."

But instead of continuing to call out the recipe instructions, E.T.'s brow suddenly furrowed in surprise. "Hey . . . weird . . . I never figured this out before. . . . *TIDINGS,* which is the answer to 52-Across, that's my middle name . . . Well, not quite, because I'm spelled differently—T-Y-D-I-N-G-S. . . . That's kind of neat, though. . . . I can call myself *Holiday news* from now on."

"And what does the E stand for?" Belle asked. She didn't expect an answer. E.T. was as secretive about the origins of his name as he was about his home life, but instead of changing the subject as he normally did, he unexpectedly scrunched up his face. "Ellicott," he mumbled, "Because of my great grandfather, Ellicott Tydings. . . . I never knew him. He was called 'Dutch.'"

"Ellicott Tydings doesn't sound like the name of someone from the Netherlands," Belle remarked, but even as she said the words, a small gong went off in her head. *Dutch,* she thought. *Of course! Maybe this mystery woman wasn't married to a man from Holland as I imagined Mr. Liebig suggested . . . Maybe Dutch was a nickname— just like E.T.* "I don't suppose your great-grandmother's maiden name was Dodge . . . ?" Belle asked after a pause. "Or . . . or Swerve, by any chance?" She grimaced as she spoke; the query sounded daffy even by her standards—as well as another major long shot.

The look E.T. gave Belle showed how completely loopy he thought the question was. "*Swerve?* You mean, like turn away to avoid from slamming into something? Like what I do on my bike when I see an icy patch . . . ? Man, and I thought Ellicott Tydings Whitman was a dorky—"

But Belle's brain had already made another startling connection, and she hurried to the window-side table where copies of the crossword recipes lay scattered among the cake ingredients. "Old Mr. Liebig couldn't remember the young woman's name . . . ," she muttered to herself as she began scanning the puzzles. "When I went to Legendary, trying to discover who'd created this book, he didn't have a clue . . . but then when he and his son brought the chocolate village to the inn, he suddenly . . ." Belle's eyes were racing through the across and down clues and solutions. "I assumed it was a surname he was recalling. . . . He said Swerve; I immediately thought he meant Dodge. . . . as if his thought process had made a natural verbal transference, because Dodge is such a solid Massachusetts name. . . . But maybe—"

"What are you talking about, Belle?" E.T. demanded. Her mumbled monologue had clearly lost him.

Belle turned to face the boy. "Maybe it was your great-grandmother who made this book, E.T. I know it's a huge, huge leap, but—"

"Huh?" E.T. squinted at this book in Belle's hand.

"What's another word for *swerve*?"

E.T. thought. "Veer?"

"And what sounds like veer?"

"Steer . . . deer . . . clear . . . near—?"

"No, silly, a woman's name."

E.T.'s mouth fell open. "V-Vera. That was my great-gran's name."

"And was her husband the man whose nickname was 'Dutch'?"

E.T. could only nod in reply while Belle beamed at him and pointed to one of the puzzles. "Look . . . here in the "ANGEL IN DISGUISE" recipe . . . read the solution to 43-Across."

"*VERA,*" E.T. said. Then he studied Belle. There was decided skepticism in his expression. "Well, sure . . . but that doesn't prove anything, because the puzzle says it's the answer to VERA *Cruz.*"

Belle ignored the argument as she began riffling through the crosswords. "And the daughter she created this for . . . is called . . . *EVA* . . . *ANITA* . . . *GRETA* . . . *LENA* . . . *PENNY* . . . *TESS*—"

"No, my grandma's Lee," E.T. admitted in a small voice. It was clear he found the name as unhip as Ellicott Tydings.

"LEE," Belle whispered in awe. "Here it is at 24-Down in "Holiday Slay Ride." "We're supposed to think the reference is to Robert E., the *Gray general* listed in the clues, but if I'm correct in my assumption—Oh wow . . . !" She gazed at E.T., her eyes glistening with tears. "I'll bet this book was made for your grandmother," she told him. "I'll just bet it was. And we're going to take it to her right now."

E.T. response to this suggestion was to stiffen his shoulders and draw away. He stared at the tabletop as he spoke. "We can't."

Belle gulped, and also drew back. "Oh, E.T . . . How dumb of me! It didn't occur to me that perhaps your grandmother isn't living—"

"Oh, she's around, all right," the boy stated as he continued to gaze fixedly at the table.

Belle's shoulders sagged in consternation and regret. *You dope!* she berated herself. *No wonder this kid doesn't talk about home. His mother's probably at odds with his grandmother; his dad's caught in the middle, and they're all crammed into one house, living too close to one another to have*

*enough breathing room to think straight. Why can't I learn
that not everything in life is peaches and cream?* Belle gently
shut the little cookbook. "Well, that's fine. . . . Maybe
you can tell your grandmother about it sometime.
When you feel like it, I mean. . . . I can keep it for you
for a while. I'm sure Mr. Mitchell and Mr. Morgan
wouldn't mind . . . or . . . or you can tell your mom and
let her decide—"

"That's just it!" E.T. burst in. "I don't have a
mom . . . or a dad. It's just Gran and me. And she
doesn't . . . well, she doesn't care about books and
things like that." He swiped manfully at his eyes while
Belle perched on a chair beside him. If he hadn't continued to stand so rigidly apart, she would have put a com-
forting arm around his thin, unhappy shoulders.

"You're being raised by your grandmother?"

"Yeah," was the unwilling answer.

"And you and your Gran don't always agree on
things?" Belle couldn't think of another way to phrase
the question. She wanted to ask about the circumstances concerning the boy's absent parents, but she
knew the timing was inappropriate; she also realized
she should remain as neutral and nonjudgmental as
possible.

In answer to the question, E.T. nodded—once. "She
just gets so . . . grouchy."

Belle thought for a moment. "Well sometimes, it's

hard for older people to raise children. . . . Sometimes, they don't have the patience they need. . . ."

E.T. considered this while Belle continued to speak.

"And, maybe your grandmother misses having your parents nearby. . . . I mean, if they're living and work- ing in another state—" *Or locked up in prison,* Belle thought, but left unsaid.

"But my dad and my mom haven't been around for a long time! They died when I was a little baby. If I don't miss them, I don't know why Gran has to!"

The lump that rose in Belle's throat forced her to take a deep and steadying breath. Her own tears of empathy wouldn't help the boy standing beside her. "I don't imagine mothers ever get over the loss of their children, E.T.," she told him, then paused, studying his face. "But you know something? You're not your dad. Whoever he was, and whatever goods things he did in his life, you're not him—and you're not supposed to be. Who you are is E.T.; and E.T.'s one terrific and smart kid—even if he doesn't like his name very much."

E.T. didn't speak for a long while, but Belle could see he was processing everything she'd said. His posture and facial expressions shifted and changed as if he were reliving a series of events.

"You know what, Belle?" he finally announced. "I think my Gran might like seeing this cookbook after all. . . . Do you think Mr. Mitchell would let her keep it—if it's really hers, I mean? And maybe we could give her this cake we're making from the book? She really loves chocolate."

"Absolutely!" Then Belle gave him the hug she'd wanted to all along. "And we'll make another one for Ms. Lionetti, how's that?"

Eighteen

INDING herself standing on the old and sloping porch of Lee Whitman's farmhouse with the crossword cookbook in one hand and the still-warm "Christmas, Current" cake in the other, Belle began having serious misgivings about the mission she'd embarked upon. The home looked cold and unwelcoming; there wasn't a hint of holiday decor in evidence; there wasn't a lamp lit or the sound of a radio or TV issuing forth; if E.T hadn't been standing staunchly at her side, she would have imagined the place deserted.

"I think it would be a good idea if you knock, Belle," he told her. "I've got my key, but Gran might not be too pleased if I just walked in with someone she's never met. I don't bring any friends over, so . . ." E.T. left the remainder of the thought unfinished while Belle produced a poor facsimile of a breezy smile and rapped loudly and energetically on the door.

The woman who opened it two minutes later could only have been E.T.'s grandmother. Although no taller than he, she had the same slight and wiry build and the same curling red hair—now noticeably gray. Her face was also gray, and hard lines had etched themselves into her cheeks. "Yes?" She didn't smile as she spoke; in fact, her expression seemed to grow even tighter when she saw her grandson.

"Mrs. Whitman, I'm Belle Graham. . . . I'm the crossword editor for the *Evening Crier,*" she added hastily, hoping the job title might provide an air of legitimacy. "I met your grandson at the Revere Inn. He was instrumental in helping my husband investigate— I should say *solve*—the theft of . . ."

In the midst of this explanation, Lee Whitman turned her stare from Belle and squinted at E.T. as if she expected him to be of little help in any situation, let alone a criminal investigation. The boy gazed back gamely, but didn't speak while his grandmother returned her focus to the woman who'd just appeared on her porch. "That Marz family," was the crisp reply. "They're plain, hard-luck people. I remember my mother telling me that when I was just a girl. She was down there a lot, helping the widow—" The words abruptly ceased, and then as jerkily began again. "I guess it was because Mama was a war widow, and she understood how hard it was to be left on your own." Then that effort also lurched to a halt. Belle could see Lee Whitman closing off every trace of emotional response. Nothing: neither the past nor future was going to cause her pain again.

"Well, your grandson was a wonderful addition to the case," Belle insisted. She then reiterated E.T.'s role, concluding with a cheery "In fact, he was the one who untangled the entire riddle when he noticed a punctuation mark no one else had."

"Is that so?" said Lee Whitman, although the remark sounded bemused rather than impressed.

"You should be very proud of him, Mrs. Whitman," Belle continued with some force. "He's an exceptionally bright boy."

But E.T. had had enough of this stalled chitchat. "Gran!" he piped up loudly. "Belle made a cake . . . a special chocolate cake—"

"As a reward for being such a help?" was the caustic reply. "Money would have been handier."

But E.T. was obviously accustomed to this cynical behavior. "No, Gran," he argued. "It's not a reward. It's a gift. For you." Then he grabbed both the cake and the crossword cookbook from Belle and thrust them toward his grandmother. "And this book's a gift, too. It's got recipes made into puzzles. . . . Belle filled in the solutions . . . well, not these actual crosswords, 'cause she made copies of them . . . but look . . ." Forcing the cake into his grandmother's hand, he opened the book. "There! See where 'Mama' is writing to her 'dear daughter who so loves chocolate'? Belle thinks that's you! 'Cause the puzzles have *TIDINGS* and *VERA* and—"

"Oh!" Lee Whitman gasped as she stared down at the page E.T. held open. "Oh my word!" Her defiant posture was gone in a trice, and she lifted her eyes to gaze in disbelief at both her grandson and at Belle. "Oh, my . . . my . . . my . . ." Finally, she took the cookbook in trembling fingers. The knifelike lines in her face had vanished, and tears were beginning to drip down her cheeks. "Where did you . . . ?" she began as E.T. turned the pages, and she gently touched each with a calloused finger as though afraid too much pressure might harm this wondrous object. "I remember Mama showing me this. . . . She was just so proud. . . . Made it during the war when Papa was . . . before Papa . . . but then the book just disappeared, and we . . . well, Mama and I never—"

"Gran," E.T. interjected with a twelve-year-old's fidgety impatience. "It's *freezing* out here. Can we come in and discuss all this history stuff where it's warm?"

"Well, Ellicott Tydings Whitman, of course you can come inside. What did you think? That I'd totally forgotten my manners, and I was going to force you and Ms. Graham to stand outside for the rest of the day? Come in . . . come in. . . ." She stood against the door, holding it wide for her grandson and Belle to enter. "And let's have some of my mama's lovely cake." But those four words put a quick end to Lee Whitman's offer. "My mama . . . ," she repeated in the barest of whispers; then she looked out into the snowy yard as though she were staring into a past chocked full of memories. But instead of regret, her expression was suffused with a bittersweet joy.

Swinging the door shut behind her, she regarded her grandson. She seemed to have grown both taller and gentler, as well as more "grandmotherly." "Mama would have been proud of you, E.T." Lee stated. "She loved words—just like you do. And she was brave, like you are, and determined, too—like you. And clever. All those smart genes missed me by a mile . . . and your daddy and mommy, too. But you ended up with every one of them."

By the time she finished this speech, Lee Whitman was beaming; and Belle could see that E.T. was beaming also. "So don't you ever forget you've got one terrific brain. Why, you can do anything you put your mind to, E.T. Anything, at all. . . . Now, tell me what you did to help out the investigation at the inn. Don't leave out one single detail. I want to feel filled up with pride. And we'll all have a piece of Belle's chocolate cake. 'Christmas, Current.' . . . It was was my favorite when I was your age."

BELLE'S eyes shone with tears as she recounted the story to Rosco that evening. They were sitting on the couch in the living room, a fire lighting up the hearth, and the two dogs curled up on the rug and basking in the warmth of the reflected blaze.

"I don't believe either of them could have imagined receiving a better Christmas present than the gift of each other," she concluded. "And to think the catalyst was such a small thing—a little, unprepossessing homemade book of dessert recipes. . . . If Mitchell hadn't found it at a yard sale and decided to add it to the inn's library . . . if I hadn't been wandering around as a useless member of Sisters-in-Stitches and asked to borrow it—"

"But he did. And you did," Rosco countered gently.

Belle nodded. "Isn't it amazing how many miracles there are in the world? We only need to stop once in a while to notice them."

"You're mine; I know that much," was Rosco quiet answer.

"I'm being serious," Belle said, but she was smiling softly as she spoke.

"So am I."

"I know. . . ."

They held each other, remaining happily silent as they watched the flames flickering upward with a radiant glow. The room was incredibly peaceful—and warm against the snowy cold of the world beyond.

"I'm really looking forward to introducing Lee to everyone at Martha's party Wednesday evening. And she's incredibly pleased to be included. You should have seen her discussing the shindig with E.T." Belle sighed; the sound was full of contentment. Then she suddenly sat straighter and chuckled with delight.

"I take it you're planning to share your private joke."

Belle smiled grew into a grin. "I was thinking what a Dickens of a time Martha's going to have solving the crossword I constructed to accompany the gift Stan bought her."

"She has to do a puzzle in order to get her present? Why not make her take the bar exam? Belle, I thought you were *helping* Stan, not making things tougher."

"It's the icing on the cake, as it were. . . . Stan found Martha a really pretty gold bracelet with a heart-shaped charm that he had engraved with the words *For My Special Friend.* He's hiding it in a box of chocolates; Karl

Liebig is foil-wrapping the bracelet so it looks like an innocent cordial cherry. That way, if Martha decides to open her gift in front of her guests, she won't be reduced to the part of blushing teenager . . . and the surprise when she unwraps it will be that much sweeter."

"A bracelet? That's it? No fancy ring? With a rock the size of Rhode Island? No bended knee and stammered question? Sara's going to pretty darn disappointed at these turn of events. Rumor has it, she's already reserved a reception hall for the nuptials."

"Well, Sara will have to learn to be patient," was Belle's rather smug reply. "Love can't be hurried."

"As proclaimed by Miss Patience herself," Rosco observed with his own wry chortle.

"Hey, I'm tackling my missing social skills in order. Learning to be patient will just have to be put on the back burner."

"May I ask what pressing 'social skill' precedes learning patience?"

"Baking." Belle beamed. "I just discovered how to make a pretty darned fabulous dessert."

"Ah, the old 'Let them eat cake' thing."

Belle gazed at her husband. "Isn't this the most wonderful coincidence, Rosco? Marie Antoinette and her mother and siblings were reunited in those two paintings—enjoying chocolate, just like Lee and her mom and E.T."

"Don't lose your head over the similarities here, Belle."

"I'm not even going to respond to that crass remark."

"I hate to break the news, but you just did."

ACROSS

1. Record label
4. Fur magnate
9. Hoop and holler
13. Tore
14. New Zealander
15. Mr. Gillis
16. "_____ April"
18. Synthetic fabric
19. "Adios!"
20. Quote ending, part 1
22. Sample
24. Mr. Idle
25. Author of quote
32. Incline
33. See 34-Across
34. With 33-Across, classic Monroe film
37. Quote ending, part 2
41. "_____ Wednesday," Resnik play
42. Miss Karenina
44. Some Southeast Asians
46. Quote ending, part 3
52. Mr. Guinness
53. Roofing support
55. Williams & O'Neill
61. Bulldogs home?
62. Unresponsive states
63. Quote ending, part 4
65. Metal on metal sound
66. 34-Across director
67. Take home
68. Penny
69. Les _____ Unis
70. 4-Down members

DOWN

1. Build
2. Wild one
3. Payment method
4. M.D.'s org.
5. Caroled
6. Oz pooch
7. Cookie sandwich
8. Expelled
9. Namesakes of "a fellow of infinite jest"
10. North Sea feeder
11. Jungle king
12. Impart
15. Column class
17. "_____ the blazes"
21. Datebook abbr.
23. Mr. Gardner
26. Slack
27. Letter add-on; abbr.
28. Mr. McQueen
29. Seventh Greek letter
30. Profit or sense lead-in
31. Mole
34. Snare
35. Not quite due?
36. _____-Cat
38. Type of cushion
39. Mr. Danson
40. Old soap? abbr.
43. Unyielding
45. Witch
47. Winter warmer?
48. No longer at it; abbr.
49. Tree decoration
50. "_____Sympathy," Anderson play
51. Reindeer reiner?

"There's Nothing Better Than a . . ."

54. Runs into
55. Charlemagne's crowning year
56. Hamlet, e.g.
57. _____, a plan, a canal, Panama
58. Worn out
59. Forum garb
60. "Beat it!"
64. Switch positions

171

Answers

🌴 *Holiday Slay Ride* 🌴

¹F	²A	³C	⁴E	⁵S	■	⁶B	⁷U	⁸L	⁹B	■	¹⁰P	¹¹R	¹²O	¹³D
¹⁴O	R	O	N	O	■	¹⁵A	S	E	A	■	¹⁶R	O	M	A
¹⁷A	T	L	A	S	■	¹⁸B	E	A	K	■	¹⁹I	T	E	M
²⁰L	I	D	S	■	²¹T	O	R	R	I	²²D	Z	O	N	E
²³S	E	C	■	²⁴L	E	O	S	■	²⁵N	I	E	■	■	■
■	■	²⁶O	²⁷C	E	A	N	■	²⁸S	G	T	·	²⁹W	³⁰H	³¹O
³²R	³³I	F	L	E	S	■	³⁴C	A	P	■	³⁵T	H	I	N
³⁶A	L	F	A	■	³⁷P	³⁸L	U	T	O	■	³⁹A	I	D	E
⁴⁰P	L	E	D	■	⁴¹O	U	T	■	⁴²W	⁴³A	L	T	E	R
⁴⁴S	S	E	■	⁴⁵D	O	G	■	⁴⁶A	D	D	L	E	■	■
■	■	⁴⁷S	O	N	■	⁴⁸A	B	E	S	■	⁴⁹S	⁵⁰O	⁵¹P	
⁵²B	⁵³R	⁵⁴O	W	N	S	⁵⁵U	G	A	R	■	⁵⁶R	U	N	E
⁵⁷R	A	N	I	■	⁵⁸A	V	E	C	■	⁵⁹P	A	G	A	N
⁶⁰A	R	E	S	■	⁶¹L	E	N	A	■	⁶²A	G	A	I	N
⁶³T	E	S	S	■	⁶⁴T	A	T	S	■	⁶⁵T	E	R	R	Y

🌴 *Angel in Disguise* 🌴

¹G	²A	³G	■	⁴M	⁵A	⁶T	■	⁷E	⁸D	⁹S	■	¹⁰G	¹¹B	¹²S
¹³O	N	A	■	¹⁴O	V	A	■	¹⁵C	E	P	■	¹⁶R	A	P
¹⁷O	T	T	■	¹⁸V	A	N	¹⁹I	L	L	A	■	²⁰E	K	E
²¹D	I	O	²²D	E	■	²³G	N	A	T	■	²⁴S	T	E	W
■	²⁵C	R	E	A	²⁶M	O	F	T	A	²⁷R	T	A	R	■
■	■	■	²⁸C	I	I	■	■	²⁹S	E	A	■	■	■	■
³⁰S	³¹U	³²P	E	R	F	³³I	³⁴N	³⁵E	■	³⁶B	Y	³⁷L	³⁸A	³⁹W
⁴⁰T	R	O	P	■	⁴¹F	R	O	N	⁴²T	■	⁴³V	E	R	A
⁴⁴A	N	I	T	⁴⁵A	■	⁴⁶E	G	G	W	⁴⁷H	I	T	E	S
■	■	■	⁴⁸I	L	⁴⁹S	■	■	⁵⁰E	A	T	■	■	■	■
■	⁵¹C	⁵²H	O	P	P	⁵³E	⁵⁴D	⁵⁵P	E	C	A	⁵⁶N	⁵⁷S	■
⁵⁸C	H	I	N	■	⁵⁹R	U	D	E	■	⁶⁰K	L	I	E	⁶¹G
⁶²R	I	D	■	⁶³T	U	B	E	P	⁶⁴A	N	■	⁶⁵C	R	O
⁶⁶A	L	E	■	⁶⁷I	C	I	■	⁶⁸U	S	E	■	⁶⁹E	V	A
⁷⁰M	D	S	■	⁷¹N	E	E	■	⁷²P	A	Y	■	⁷³R	E	L

🌴 Christmas, Current 🌴

1 G	2 A	3 M	4 E	5 R	█	█	6 T	7 A	8 B	█	9 C	10 O	11 B
12 O	B	E	R	13 O	N	█	14 A	L	L	█	15 O	A	R
16 B	O	U	R	B	17 O	N	█	18 L	E	O	█	19 R	T	E
20 S	M	S	█	21 B	L	A	22 C	K	C	O	23 F	F	E	E
█	24 B	E	25 N	E	A	T	H	█	26 P	O	U	N	D
█	█	27 E	R	N	█	28 O	29 C	30 H	E	R	█	█
31 S	32 P	33 A	T	S	█	34 C	U	R	R	A	N	35 T	36 S	37 S
38 E	G	G	█	39 F	40 R	O	T	H	█	41 O	H	O
42 M	A	T	43 E	44 R	I	A	L	█	45 B	46 B	G	U	N
█	47 N	O	R	M	A	█	48 I	R	E
49 S	50 A	51 R	O	S	█	52 T	53 I	D	I	N	G	54 S	55 S
56 U	N	S	57 W	58 E	E	T	E	N	E	D	█	59 L	A	I	60
61 G	O	V	█	62 O	D	E	█	63 N	A	G	64 G	I	N	G
65 A	L	P	█	66 P	I	N	S	█	67 L	E	A	N	T	O
68 R	E	S	█	69 L	A	T	█	70 S	I	T	A	R

❦ "There's Nothing Better Than a . . ." ❦

1 E	2 M	3 I	■	4 A	5 S	6 T	7 O	8 R	■	■	9 Y	10 E	11 L	12 L
13 R	A	N	■	14 M	A	O	R	I	■	15 D	O	B	I	E
16 E	N	C	17 H	A	N	T	E	D	■	18 O	R	L	O	N
19 C	I	A	O	■	20 G	O	O	D	21 F	R	I	E	N	D
22 T	A	S	T	23 E	■	■	24 E	R	I	C	■	■	■	■
■	25 C	H	A	R	26 L	27 E	28 S	■	D	I	C	29 K	30 E	31 N S...
■	■	■	32 S	L	A	N	T	■	■	33 S	T	O	P	
34 B	35 U	36 S	■	37 E	X	C	E	38 P	39 T	40 A	■	41 A	N	Y
42 A	N	N	43 A	■	■	■	44 V	I	E	T	45 S	■	■	■
46 G	O	O	D	47 F	48 R	49 I	E	N	D	W	I	50 T	51 H	
■	■	■	52 A	L	E	C	■	■	■	53 T	B	E	A	54 M
55 D	56 R	57 A	M	A	T	I	S	58 T	59 S	■	61 Y	A	L	E
62 C	O	M	A	S	■	63 C	H	O	C	64 O	L	A	T	E
65 C	L	A	N	K	■	66 L	O	G	A	N	■	67 N	E	T
68 C	E	N	T	■	69 E	T	A	T	S	■	70 D	R	S	